I0584643

FROZEN WATERS

KARI LEE HARMON

OLIVER HEBER BOOKS

All rights reserved.

No part of this publication may be sold, copied, distributed, reproduced or transmitted in any form or by any means, mechanical or digital, including photocopying and recording or by any information storage and retrieval system without the prior written permission of both the publisher, Oliver Heber Books and the author, Kari Lee Townsend, except in the case of brief quotations embodied in critical articles and reviews.

PUBLISHER'S NOTE: This is a work of fiction. Names, characters, places, and incidents either are the product of the author's imagination or are used fictitiously. Any resemblance to actual persons, living or dead, business establishments, events, or locales is entirely coincidental.

Copyright © Kari Lee Townsend

Published by Oliver-Heber Books

0 9 8 7 6 5 4 3 2 1

There's nothing quite like having a sister. To my sister, Debbie Russo. Thank you for always being there for me, listening to me, and weathering our storms together. I'm so lucky to have you in my life. Love you lots. And to all the sisters out there who might be lost in a storm either physically or emotionally, just know you're not alone.

"HEY, CHARLIE, I'LL HAVE A BEER." Emma Ross flagged down the bartender at True North Tavern in Norfolk, Virginia.

Pop music filtered through the sound system while conversations hummed and silverware clanked against dishes. People were eating fancy seafood she couldn't quite identify. Her stomach rumbled but not for that. Looking around the trendy bar and restaurant overlooking the Atlantic Ocean, she took in the clientele. Professionals, military officers, and college students. A far cry from The Claw, her family's waterfront pub in northern Maine.

The nautical themed pub with its dim lighting and cozy ambiance would be filled with townies, fishing boat captains, and their crews right about now, eating fried clams, lobster tails soaked in butter, and king crab legs. She could almost smell it. Her mouth watered as a pang of nostalgia hit her. They would be singing along to classic rock from a local singer playing guitar on a stool in the corner while they watched a reality fishing show on a big screen TV above the bar.

Her brother, Jack, lived in the apartment above the pub while her parents owned an old colonial house in town. He helped them run the pub, planning to take it over when they retired, and he ran a snowplow business during the off season when business was slow.

Emma smiled fondly for a moment before her lips tipped down as she thought of home. She hadn't been back since she'd graduated college from Virginia Tech as a meteorologist, but it wasn't her fault. Work kept her busy, she thought, trying to convince herself that her absence was because of the job and not her past.

"Earth to Emma. Where'd you go?" Harvey Cooper Jones sat on the barstool beside her, pushing his glasses farther up his nose, then taking a sip of his red wine.

"Sorry, Harvey, I was daydreaming." She pulled the sleeves of her sweater down over her hands so just her fingers were sticking out.

"It's good to dream. All we do is work." He swirled the deep red liquid in his glass while staring into the contents as if mesmerized. "We could all use some R& R. This hurricane season had to be one of the most active on record."

"Amen to that, my friend." She played with the label on her beer bottle, peeling the edges up. Her version of a fidget device. She was always restless when she wasn't working. It gave her too much time to think and being alone with her thoughts was a scary place for her. "And what's with these crazy winter storms up and down the coast?" she continued. "Winters are getting shorter, summers are getting hotter, storms are getting worse. I swear global warming is going to do us all in one day."

"Don't get me wrong, I love storm chasing." His honey brown gaze met hers and held. "The work we do helps save lives, but we haven't had any downtime in far too many months to count. I'm exhausted. Aren't you?"

She lifted one shoulder. "It's part of the job."

Emma had met Harvey in college. He was a research

technology guy who knew how to build and operate all sorts of meteorological equipment. He looked like that superhero, Black Panther, but the man was a lover not a fighter.

A petite woman with pink hair, lavender eyes, and tattoos slowly walked toward them, twirling a set of keys around her finger. A sly grin spread across her face and a sparkle shined bright in her eyes.

Harvey groaned. "Not again, Jo. Please tell me you didn't."

She shrugged. "I can't help it that people underestimate me, Harv."

"This isn't the fifties, JoJo. You can't keep racing people for pink slips." Emma shook her head and took a sip of her beer while Harvey slid the glass of scotch he'd ordered for JoJo in front of her seat, his turtleneck straining at the seams.

"A deal's a deal." She wore a t-shirt and jeans, even though it was freezing out, but she liked to show off her pride and joy—the gator tattoo on her forearm. "Besides, no one's gonna mess with me when they see me with my boy Harv here." She slapped his bulging bicep then sat down on the barstool next to him and tossed back her drink, shooting him a wink.

Harvey just rolled his eyes.

Harvey had been roommates with JoJo's brother in college. After Emma had recruited him for her storm chasing team, he'd told her he had the perfect driver in mind. JoJo Coletrain was from the Louisiana bayou and could drive and fix anything with an engine like no one he'd ever seen. She was fearless in the face of any storm, but she was terrified of lightning.

JoJo drove The Beast, their storm chasing vehicle she'd built from scratch, but didn't venture outside of it. Harvey took the pictures, shot the 3D video footage, and placed the probes outside in front of the storm's path. Emma read the radar, predicted where the storms would hit, and navigated their every move. They made one hell of a team, but even Emma could admit they would get burned out if they kept up at this pace.

"The National Weather Service has issued a warning for a Nor'easter to hit Maine in the next two days. With hurricane force winds and dropping temperatures, a blizzard is expected to leave a couple feet of snow in its wake if it moves inland. Gather your supplies, hunker down, and stay safe. Coldwater Cove is one town I would *not* want to be near come this weekend," the news weatherman stated from the TV broadcast, looking grave.

Emma's gaze locked on the TV screen. "That storm watch just became a storm warning. You guys up for another chase?" A watch was issued two to four days in advance, but a warning meant in twelve to twenty-four hours a storm was imminent.

Harvey's eyes followed Emma's. "Oh, Em, that's about as far north up the coast as we can go. It would take us thirteen or more hours to drive The Beast. We'd have to leave first thing tomorrow morning if we wanted to beat the storm. What happened to our R&R?"

"I gotta say I agree with Harv on this one, Em. The Beast needs a few repairs, and we're riding on fumes." JoJo squinted at the TV screen. "That radar looks pretty intense, and lack of sleep makes a person sloppy. Sloppy and storm chasing don't mix. You know that. I say we sit this one out."

Emma was used to working as a team. She'd never chased a storm alone. She needed their help, but she understood their hesitancy. They didn't know that she didn't have the luxury of not chasing this particular storm. Not after what had happened.

She stood and paid the bill for all of their drinks. "These are on me. Stay and enjoy yourselves."

"Where are you going?" Harvey arched a thick black eyebrow.

"To chase a storm."

"You're seriously going to go alone?" JoJo frowned.

Emma slipped her puffer jacket on and nodded once as she picked up her purse and headed for the door.

"Wait," Harvey hollered from behind her. "Why are you so hell bent on chasing this particular storm?"

Emma glanced one more time at the TV screen above the bar before looking back at them both. "Because Coldwater Cove is my home."

***

GUNNER NASH STOOD on the dock of the marina in Coldwater Cove and stared out over the dark churning water, inhaling the scent of salt and sea. The sky was clear, but the air carried an icy chill like nothing he'd ever felt. It penetrated deep to the bone, and he welcomed the numbness that came along with that.

Gunner had been to and seen a lot of places, but there was something majestic and raw about Maine. Eerie almost. The rugged coastline with jagged rocks and snow-covered forests swept down to the sea, and peninsulas reached out like crooked fingers threatening to pull you in. Cliffs that were peppered with rocky shores and dotted with lighthouses stretched along both sides of the shoreline as far as the eye could see.

The marina remained open in the winter, but not many boats were docked. The town was a small seaside fishing village in the northern part of Maine with a humid continental climate. The winters were cold and snowy while the summers were warm. Direct strikes from hurricanes and tropical storms from June through November were rare this far north because of the cooler Atlantic waters, but nor'easters could hit between November and March.

When they hit in the winter months, they were the most severe.

As a Navy Seal, Gunner knew all of this, but he didn't care. After what he'd been through, he welcomed the brutal winter. The dark and desolate ghost town, with the sun rising and setting early this far north, was exactly what he needed right now. He needed to be alone to decompress after his last mission. His superior officer had ordered him to take R&R and get his head on straight.

As if that was possible.

He clenched his teeth together, pushing the memories away, and glanced at his watch. Dinner time. No wonder his stomach was growling. His gaze passed the Harbormaster's office and landed on The Claw, a waterfront pub that looked right up his alley. He headed in that direction. As he drew near, he heard the unmistakable rasp of southern rock music coming from inside and knew he'd made the right decision.

Gunner stepped through the front door of The Claw, and all eyes turned to him. After an uncomfortable moment, people went back to their conversations, and he relaxed as much as he possibly could. He'd been on alert and ready for action for years and didn't know how to be any other way. Feeling the warmth of a fire burning in one corner, he gravitated in that direction. Scanning the room, he took in the big, burly young man with a long brown beard playing a guitar and singing in the other corner.

Gunner looked around at the rustic décor, filled with all sorts of antique nautical paraphernalia. The place wasn't busy because most of the town hibernated in the winter and tourists were rare. He'd done his homework before coming here, wanting the isolation. Based on the conversations humming around the room, there were a few regulars talking about the weather and the ski season. They had high hopes for this year's young athletes, both at the high school and up at the academy, to put Coldwater Cove on the map.

Gunner headed for the bar.

"Head's up, Eugene." A man who looked to be in his thirties, with thick dirty blond hair and sea-green eyes, slid a draft beer to an old man of the sea, sporting a long white beard and fishing cap.

"Much obliged, Jack." The old man caught the draft without spilling a drop and then took a sip. He looked up and his eyes widened.

Gunner sat a couple seats down, taking off his olive-green parka and draping it across the back of the barstool.

"You're not from around these parts," the man named Eugene said.

"Nope." Gunner glanced at the man.

"How tall are ya, Son?" Eugene squinted. "You've gotta be well over six foot."

"Six-five."

"Military?"

"Navy Seal."

"I could tell by the haircut."

Gunner nodded once.

"Not much of a talker, are ya?" The old man studied him as he chewed on a toothpick.

Gunner shrugged.

"Don't mind Eugene. He talks enough for all of us." The bartender gave the old man a meaningful look.

Eugene scowled then went back to his beer.

The bartender held out his hand. "Jack Ross. My family owns this pub."

"Gunner Nash." He shook Jack's hand.

"What can I get you, Gunner?" Jack asked.

"Whiskey neat."

Jack arched a blond eyebrow. "That kind of day?"

Gunner met his eyes. "Aren't they all?"

The National Weather Bulletin flashed across the big screen TV hanging above the bar, warning the nor'easter was strengthening and looking to make a direct impact on the Cove. Suggestions were starting to roll out about evacuating the town if things got worse, inciting mutters of disapproval from the pub's occupants.

Jack slid a bowl of steaming clam chowder and a hunk of sourdough bread in front of Gunner. "It's on the house."

This time Gunner raised a brow.

"The Claw has the best chowder in three counties." Jack grinned. "That has to help improve your day."

Gunner nodded his thanks and dug in. He hadn't realized how hungry he was after arriving just that morning in town. He liked being in control and didn't want to be without a car or his pack, so he'd driven his truck from coast to coast, stopping only when necessary. Besides, he liked seeing the country along the way, and weather of any kind didn't scare him.

He was trained to survive the worst.

"That's storm's gonna hit early," Eugene said. "I can feel it in my bones." He massaged his large hands, gnarled from years of dedication to the sea, as he looked at Gunner. "Don't know why you'd want to come to Coldwater Cove outside tourist season, especially with this monster storm heading our way."

"*You're* not leaving," Gunner pointed out as he finished his bowl of soup and sipped his whiskey.

"Bah, you won't find any of us regulars who call this small-town home willing to leave. People from Maine aren't like regular folks. We're built for storms. And I, for one, am too old and weathered to change my ways. But you just got here." He narrowed his eyes. "You got a death wish or somethin'?"

Gunner stared down at the amber liquid in his glass. "Or something."

Jack's phone vibrated. He frowned at it before sighing as he answered. "Before you even start, we're not leaving."

He shook his head as he listened to the person on the other end of the line.

"Mom and Dad have a storm cellar in their basement in town, and I've boarded up the windows on my apartment above The Claw. We'll take our chances, Emma."

His jaw hardened as he listened to her talk.

"Well, maybe you should have thought of that before leaving Coldwater Cove. You haven't been back in years, Em. They miss you."

He looked sad as he listened again.

"I hope your *job* makes you happy." Jack hung up and then tossed his phone in a drawer behind the bar, then poured himself a shot of whiskey. He met Gunner's eyes and saluted him before tossing the brown liquid back.

The door to The Claw flew open on a gust of wind, and in walked another man who didn't look like he belonged there. He wore designer jeans, a black wool coat, and black leather boots. His pale blonde hair was slicked back, not moving an inch as his piercing light blue eyes searched the room with anger.

The rumbling conversation came to a halt, even the singer stopped singing.

"Where's Ford Clark?" the man ground out with a thick, foreign accent.

"What's this about, Haanes?" Jack asked.

"My business is between the Clarks and myself."

"I don't want any trouble in my family's pub. The last time you two were here, your brawl cost me more than insurance was willing to pay."

"He deserved it then, and he deserves it even more now."

"Don't make me come around this bar and escort you out." Jack swung his dishtowel over his shoulder. "You shouldn't be in town. It's not safe."

"Apparently no place is safe around these parts." Haanes lost some of his anger, looking worried and visibly upset.

"Ford and Betty went on up the mountain to fetch their daughter, Mandy, from the ski academy on account of the storm headed our way," Eugene spouted off, then rubbed his knees. "It's gonna be a doozy."

"Shouldn't you be doing the same thing with your daughter, Westergaard?" Jack asked. "I'm sure the academy will evacuate until things blow over."

"I was in the US on business. As soon as I saw the weather report, I flew my private jet here from NY. Only problem is, Astrid is missing." His gaze hardened once more. "I know the Clarks are behind it. They're trying to get rid of Mandy's competition because Astrid has been beating her at the junior regional races. I'll be damned if I'll let them ruin my daughter's chances of making the Olympic team after nationals. But first, I have to find her."

Conversations hummed and phone calls were being made.

"Storm or no storm, I'm not leaving until I get some answers and find my daughter."

Emma flew to Maine and rented a car to get to Coldwater Cove faster. Since her team wasn't with her, she would go it alone. Her family was more stubborn than she was, and she couldn't risk any of them dying.

She knew storms.

She could at least keep them safe, and while she was here, she would implement her team's new anemometer to measure the wind speeds. She couldn't sit by during a storm of any kind and not do her part to gather data to better understand these storms so they could improve warning times. Early warnings were essential to fewer casualties, and that was Emma's primary motivation and goal.

"Emma! I can't believe you're really here." Her mother flew through the doors of the local diner, The Lost Horizon.

The owner was Harry Smith, a photographer Emma had gone to high school with. He'd been kind of a recluse back then. He spent a lot of time in the woods, which had apparently paid off. The walls were covered with gorgeous pictures of the Cove during all four seasons at various times of the day. He'd gotten really good at photography over the years, capturing all the moods of the Cove and the people who lived here.

Emma inhaled her mother, Dori's, mint and cloves scent from all the time she spent in the kitchen at the restaurant. Hugging her mother made her feel comforted and brought back memories of her childhood. Emma was the spitting image of her mother. Her embrace around Emma tightened, and she didn't let go for a long time.

Emma's father, Ben, was bald with kind gray eyes. The moment her mother finally let go, her father's eyes misted up as he pulled Emma into a huge bear hug. He'd always been a big 'ole teddy bear. She closed her eyes and let herself sink into his comforting embrace, breathing in his Old Spice aftershave.

"There's my girl," he rumbled against the top of her head, squeezing tighter. "It's been too long."

"I know." Emma wiped her eyes and then stepped out of his embrace, taking a deep shaky breath. They sat down at a table and shared a moment of silence as the waitress brought them coffee. "Work really has kept me busy, but I could have made the time," Emma admitted. "It's just been hard for me." She took a sip of coffee. "This whole town brings back so many painful memories."

"Good ones, too, I hope." Her mother smiled tenderly.

Emma nodded past the lump in her throat. "Jack's angry."

"That's because he misses his little sister." Her father's eyes filled with compassion. "He'll get over it. The point is, you're here now. I know it's because of the storm, but we'll take having you home any way we can get it."

Emma felt their disappointment in her as well as their gratitude. She had missed them so much, but she couldn't stay. The moment the storm was over, she would leave again. She had to. Staying would bring back the nightmares and panic attacks, making her feel helpless. Researching storms eased her guilt and gave her a sense of purpose.

"You're right." Emma looked them both in the eye. "I am home because of the storm, but not because I want to cover it. I've covered plenty this year, and this one is looking fierce. I'm worried about you guys. A storm this bad hasn't hit the Cove since…"

"It's okay, honey." Her mother patted her hand.

"No, it's not." Emma's voice wobbled, and she swallowed down her emotions. She had to get through to them somehow. "You guys don't know the things I know about storms. If you won't take the expert's advice to evacuate, then I'm going to ride it out with you and make sure you're all safe."

"We have plenty of room at the house. At least stay with us." Her father looked at her pleadingly.

"I can't," she responded a bit too quickly, and then took a deep breath. "You know why." She shook her head over and over. "I just can't."

"Okay, Bean." He squeezed her shoulder. "It's okay."

Emma stood. "I'll catch up with you guys later." She glanced at the TV on the wall. "The radar shows the winds are about to pick up, and I want to get my equipment in place before that happens."

"Please be careful." Her mother gripped her hand. "I can't lose you, too."

* * *

EMMA PUT ON LONG UNDERWEAR, jeans, a wool sweater, and her red parka. Red was always her color of choice so she wouldn't get lost in a storm. People would see her if she got into trouble, and that was the point. Donning her hat and gloves, she grabbed her anemometer, camera, and binoculars and carefully placed them into her backpack with her other essential supplies. Storms were unpredictable.

She'd learned over the years to always be prepared for anything.

Slipping on her pack, she walked out of her hotel room door while looking at the radar on her phone, then she ran smack into a man heading into the room across the hall. He steadied her and stepped back. She had to look up. Way up.

Holy hurricane, she hadn't been prepared for *that*.

He was so tall, and she'd never seen someone with muscles that big straining through his ribbed long-sleeve shirt. He was bigger than Harvey, and she hadn't thought that was possible. He looked like he had a light brown, clean-cut style haircut that was a little longer on the top, hypnotic hazel eyes, and a smooth-shaven chiseled face with a cleft in his chin.

Emma stared at him with her mouth agape.

"You okay?" he asked with a deep voice, his brow creasing.

"Fine. I'm fine. Just fine," she stammered, readjusting her pack. "Thank you, but I have to run." She could feel her face flame and ears burn hot as she left him staring at her oddly in the hallway. Strange, but she could still feel her nerves hum from his touch, while the smell of soap, the sea, and a musk she was certain belonged only to him lingered in her nose.

Pick up the pace, Woman.

Emma didn't stop moving until she exited the hotel. Coldwater Commons was just down the street from the Coldwater Community Center in the heart of town and not that long of a walk to reach the marina, but if the winds picked up, she would be in trouble. So, she stashed her pack in her rental car and headed toward the marina. She glanced in the rear-view mirror. It wasn't like he was going to follow her, but she couldn't help wondering who he was.

He *definitely* wasn't a local.

No man should look that gorgeous. She shook off her thoughts. She wasn't in the market for a man. Her career didn't lend itself to a healthy relationship. A fling...maybe. She jerked the car's steering wheel, almost running off the road. That was her answer right there. No time to lose focus with a monster storm headed their way.

She reached the marina and parked. No one was around except the local business owners and the harbormaster. Most people who enjoyed winter activities were inland ice fishing on lakes, snowmobiling, dog sledding, cross country skiing, and snow shoeing. But with the storm zeroing in on them, a few people had evacuated, but most were simply hunkering down in their boarded-up homes with their supplies.

Emma stepped out of the car to wind gusts that were definitely higher than yesterday. She retrieved her pack and pulled out her compact high-speed anemometer. Holding it high, it measured the wind speed. Checking the reading, the wind was already at thirty miles per hour.

Pulling out her binoculars, she looked at the waves mimicking the dread churning in her stomach. If she had to make a guess, they appeared to be around twelve feet already, which made sense at this wind speed. If this nor'easter escalated like the National Weather Bureau was predicting, it would come ashore with hurricane force winds at seventy-four miles per hour minimum. Waves could be as much as forty feet or more.

Damage to the Cove could be tremendous.

Emma glanced at The Claw. At least they'd boarded

up the windows but worry still filled her gut. Why wouldn't they listen to her? If anything happened to them, she couldn't live with herself. She had to do something, and to start, she would do her part before the storm came ashore. It was predicted to hit in the next day or two.

She placed a few scientific probes strategically so they would be picked up by the wind as the storm came ashore. Next, she snapped some pictures with her high-powered camera and took some videos. Storing her belongings in her car, she headed inland toward one of Coldwater's many parks. She *needed* to measure the snowfall before the blizzard hit and check the thickness of the ice, especially here.

She had to admit, she missed her team at a time like this.

Glancing at the sky, she felt reassured she had time. It hadn't started snowing yet. Her brother was most likely getting his trucks ready.

She missed her brother, but she dreaded seeing him.

Jack had made his anger at her perfectly clear. Pulling into the park, she parked her car and gathered her supplies. Donning snowshoes, she headed into the woods. Emma stuck to the main trail. In no time at all, she had ventured deep into the heart of the woods and didn't stop until she reached the lake.

Her heart pinched, and she realized this was harder than she had thought it would be.

Pushing back any memories that tried to crush her, she reminded herself it had been years. This was a different day, and she was a different person. A stronger person. She could do this. Retrieving her yard stick, she measured the snow. Just about one foot. She puckered her brow. If the blizzard dumped two or three feet of snow, it was going to take the entire town to dig out.

The Cove hadn't had a storm this big in many years. They'd been lucky.

Every instinct within her told her their luck was about to run out.

Emma glanced around. Just as she thought. No ice-fishers were present at this lake, and hopefully not at any others. Although the lake was pretty big. They could be further down. Drilling a small hole, she measured the ice. Eight inches. Strong enough to hold her. She donned her pack and ventured further out on the ice as the wind picked up, making it difficult to walk. The first flakes of snow started to fall. Stopping to take a few videos and pictures, she pulled her camera away and squinted off into the distance.

"What the hell?" she mumbled out loud to herself. Bears hibernated this time of year. Chewing the inside of her cheek, she looked back through the lens and zoomed in, then sucked in a breath.

That was no animal.

Maybe there really were ice fishermen out there. She couldn't quite tell, but it looked like three bodies moving across the ice. A sudden gust blew a veil of white, thick enough to hide their shadows. For a second, she wondered if she'd imagined them. When the wind settled, their figures reappeared as snow continued to fall at a furious pace.

Glancing at the sky, she cursed under her breath. Dammit! Her prediction had been off. The storm was hitting early. They needed to get to safety, but they were moving away from the trails and further across the ice, heading deeper into the woods.

"Hey! Stop!" she shouted and waved her arms, trying to catch them before they disappeared. "A storm's coming! You need to get to safety!" She kept shouting over and over until they finally stopped.

Pulling out her camera, she zoomed up and looked

through the lens, snapping off several shots. It looked like two men and a girl, but she couldn't be sure. Stowing her camera away, she grabbed her binoculars. One of the men pulled out a pair of binoculars and looked back at her, said something to the other man who then pulled out a...

Emma's heart thundered in her chest.

She dropped her binoculars and turned around to run just as a bullet whizzed by her, followed by the sound of the shot echoing off the ice. Her snowshoes were great in the snow and good on the ice, but not so good for running. She slipped and slid her way toward the shore when a second shot ripped through her parka.

Hearing the sound of the shot moments later, she realized the bullet had struck her arm. Tumbling to the ice, she cried out in pain. She held her arm and rolled over, her heart pounding loudly in her ears. What was happening? Who were these people? Oh no....

They were headed in her direction with weapons raised.

* * *

GUNNER SAT on a stool in his pop-up shanty. He hadn't caught a single fish. Given the storm that had just started, based on the persistent wind beating his tent, he reasoned even the fish were hiding. He decided to call it a day and started packing up his belongings.

As a Navy Seal, he knew survival, but even he knew it wasn't wise to get caught in this monster if it really did turn out to be a blizzard. Then again, he wasn't always wise. After what had happened, he had survivor's guilt. His superior had called him reckless and told him to see a shrink.

He'd gone fishing instead.

Gunner had just finished packing up his gear when he heard the unmistakable sound of a gunshot, followed quickly by a second. Every fiber of his being went on alert. He dropped down low and reached for the gun he was always packing. For a moment, he was back in Mexico, his ears ringing and heartbeat erratic. He had to force himself to take several deep breaths.

Dammit!

He'd come to Coldwater Cove to get away from the things that caused his PTSD to flare up. Things like guns, violence...death. It wasn't hunting season. It was a winter storm. Maybe someone was in trouble and fired shots for help. No matter what had happened to him, he was a protector.

He had to help.

Toting his large pack, he made his way toward the sound of the gunshots, keeping to the trees along the shore and staying out of sight out of habit. That old rascal had been right. The storm had hit early. Snow was coming down heavy now. The sound of voices carried on the wind across the ice. Instinct told him to assess the situation before making his presence known. Moments later, he was glad he did.

The woman from the hotel.

He'd recognize that bright red puffy coat anywhere. What the hell was she doing laying on the ice, deep in the woods alone with a storm starting? A movement caught his eye. He looked beyond her and saw a couple people moving across the ice in her direction. He dug in his pack and pulled out his binoculars in time to see one man take a knee and lift a gun.

They weren't in trouble....

She was.

He didn't think; he reacted by firing off a shot in their direction. The man with the gun fell over. A direct hit but not a kill shot. He couldn't be sure but it looked like another man pulled him to his feet, then they headed in the other direction across the ice.

Adrenaline rushed through his veins. He didn't waste any time making his way out to the woman, but the strong winds were making it more difficult to walk. Snowflakes stuck to his hat, and ice crystals formed on his nose hairs and eyelashes. He cursed when he reached her. She was covered with snow and looked paler by the second. She'd been hit, her blood blending in with her red parka. He dropped to his knees and examined her arm.

Her eyes flew open, the sea-green color sucker punching him the same as it had in the hotel when they'd collided. She was a good foot shorter than him, and her unmistakable scent of peppermint still lingered.

"You!" She gasped as her eyes widened. "What are you doing out here?"

"I could ask you the same thing." He pulled his supplies out of his pack and wrapped a bandage around her arm right over her coat.

"I'm a meteorologist. Storms are my thing." She eyed him suspiciously. "You just happen to have medical supplies with you?"

"I'm a Navy Seal." His gaze met hers. "Survival is *my* thing."

She looked at his waist, saw his gun, and gasped. "Did you shoot at me?"

He arched an eyebrow. "I saved you. You're welcome."

"Thank you, of course, but we need to get back to town ASAP and report this to search and rescue."

"More like the police."

"I don't care about me. They're going to die if they stay out in this storm."

"Let me get this straight." He helped her to her feet. "You want to save the people who shot at you."

"No." She swiped her hand through the air and blew out a frustrated breath. "I want to save the teenaged girl they have with them. I saw a missing teen on a flyer in the diner just this morning. I have to check my camera footage, but I'm pretty sure that's her."

"I didn't see any girl. The only thing you're doing is seeing a doctor." He studied her pupils before she rolled her eyes. "You obviously knocked the sense out of yourself when you hit the ice."

She started to protest, so he lifted her into his arms and started walking. Finally, something that turned off that motor mouth of hers. Only problem was, it turned on something inside of him he'd thought he had permanently buried.

What the hell had he gotten himself into?

3

Shit!

How the hell had things gotten so fucked up?

Anger consumed every fiber of my being. Stupid incompetent fools. They had one job—be gone with the girl before the storm hit. It didn't take a genius to pull that off, but obviously neither of them had a brain.

I stood in the corner of the community center, listening, watching, trying to act normal.

Half the town had gathered there to ride out the storm. The noise level had died down considerably the second Emma Ross and the giant beside her had burst through the door. They immediately sought out the sheriff and were telling their story. Anyone within earshot could hear what was going on.

Two men and a teenaged girl were out on the ice. She'd tried to help them, but they shot at her and then ran into the woods. Dammit! She was trying to convince the sheriff to track them down. This was bad. My mind whirled with thoughts of what I would do. What I *could* do. I tried not to clench my jaw.

I didn't need anyone seeing my reaction and suspecting I was involved in any way.

The bitch kept rambling on and on. I wanted to shut

her up, stuff something in her mouth or punch her in the face and knock her out, but the room was full of people. She said she recognized the girl from the pictures on the wall in the diner.

Goddamned nor'easter.

Her father was in the US on business and had his private jet at his disposal. He never would have come to the Cove to evacuate his daughter and fly her back to Scandinavia if the weather had cooperated. That was the shitty part of living in Maine. The fucking weather was always unpredictable.

What the hell was Emma Ross doing back in town, anyway?

She didn't live here anymore. Did she really have to chase *every* storm? Wasn't she supposed to stick to Tornado Alley? Of course, she couldn't be a normal storm chaser. *Oh hell.* Emma's words cut through my thoughts. She'd just said she had taken pictures of the three of them as proof.

Pictures!

Christ! If this was traced back to me, someone was going to pay. I would see to it myself. I wandered casually around the room, inching closer to where she stood, so I could see the pictures she'd just showed the sheriff. She'd set them on the stage behind her. No one paid any attention to me as I stole a glance.

Relief surged through me. At least the dumb fucks were bundled up, making it impossible to identify them. I'd purposely chosen outsiders for their help with my plan, but they weren't the brightest. And then there was the girl. There was no mistaking her signature snow gear to know who she was. With all her ski endorsements, she was a local celebrity, and her powerful rich daddy was stirring up trouble by demanding answers.

I knew taking this girl would be a risk, but it was worth it if the plan succeeded.

I had to do something to stop anyone from finding them. Whatever it took. I clenched my hands into fists and fought the urge to wrap them around Emma's throat and rip out her annoying vocal chords. I had too much to lose.

Rage filled my gaze as I stared at her in silence.

* * *

"YOU HAVE TO GO AFTER THEM," Emma pleaded with the sheriff hours later.

Gunner had taken her to be checked out by a doctor, and only after she developed her film and proved to him there was a teenager involved, did he take her to see the sheriff. Even though the bad guys had headed in the opposite direction, Emma couldn't shake the feeling that she was being watched. She rubbed her chilled hands together as she looked around the community center. Everyone was staring at her, hanging on her words. She knew most of them from her childhood, but there were a few new people since she'd left.

She shrugged off her uneasiness and focused on the sheriff.

Sheriff Trent West was a former marine turned FBI. He'd been undercover in the Cove as a delivery man a while back, helping to solve a cold case and clear his father's name. After falling for Stacy Buchanan, the daughter of the cold case victim, he'd stayed in town and become the new sheriff. While Stacy, a tall former professional swimmer with wild red curly hair, gave up a job with ESPN to stay in town to be there for her ailing father. She was now the new sports journalist and swim coach.

Stacy was all over this story since Astrid Westergaard had gone missing. Stacy's mother was mayor years ago and had been a big advocate for helping young athletes. Stacy was carrying on in her mother's footsteps, but even she agreed with her now husband Trent on the dangers of this particular nor'easter.

"Emma, you of all people know what this storm is capable of," Stacy said gently, responding to Emma's statement. "Your own brother reported the initial storm surge has already done considerable damage to the Cove. Now that it's moved inland, we're getting buried in blizzard snow. We don't need to put any other lives in danger."

Emma knew in her rational mind that Stacy was right, but her heart begged her to do something. She couldn't witness another person lose their life to a storm on her watch. Especially another teenaged girl.

This particular storm had originated as a low-pressure system formed off the shore between North Carolina and Massachusetts. As it moved up the coast, the difference in temperature between the cold polar air mass and the warmer air over the water brought heavy rain with hurricane force winds and now blizzard conditions. Nor'easters were most intense and dangerous during this time of year. Emma set her jaw in determination.

That didn't mean it couldn't be survived if you knew what you were doing.

"Look, I understand your desire to rescue this girl no matter the cost, given your history, but my hands are tied." Trent broke through Emma's thoughts. "The blizzard is raging now. There's no way I'm going to risk anyone venturing out into the woods to search and rescue them. There's zero visibility, and we would lose a lot more people. We'll have to wait until the storm blows over." Sheriff West was nearly as big as Gunner and just as tough, but he was by-the-book and all about safety.

"I understand what you're saying, but how is that fair? An innocent young girl is out there with those thugs. She must be terrified. Her life is just as important as ours. We can't sit back and do nothing." Emma stood beside Gunner at the edge of the stage, talking to the sheriff and Stacy.

"The woods are full of cabins. Everyone looks out for each other around here, and no one locks their doors. You must remember that, I'm sure. When they close them up for winter, they leave them stocked and unlocked in case of emergencies just like this," Stacy added, trying to reassure her and everyone else. "I'm sure they'll find shelter to ride out the storm, and when the weather clears, we'll go after them."

"Until then, we'll do what we can to help the people in town." Trent looked around the room as more of the locals found their way inside.

The storm had cut the town's power. With a blizzard, you had to worry about pipes freezing, hypothermia setting in, carbon monoxide poisoning, heart attacks from over-exertion, etc. Anyone without a generator had gathered at the community center to shelter in place. Tables were set up for people to sit at, as well as tents and cots scattered about in areas to sleep. Food and supplies had been stocked in advance of the storm.

The hotel where Emma and Gunner were staying had a generator, but there were no rooms left, so the community center would handle the overflow. The sheriff had been organizing rescue teams for people stranded in their homes with no power or heat.

"This isn't just a lost girl in the woods." Emma stared him down. "She was definitely kidnapped by two very bad men. Who's to say they won't kill her before the storm lets up?"

"They obviously took her for a reason." It was clear Trent was trying to calm Emma, using his former FBI reasoning skills. "If they wanted her dead, they would have killed her already. I don't want anyone doing anything crazy." He stared right back at her, using his cop intimidation skills. "Am I clear?"

Everything he said made sense, but she couldn't let it go. She pushed her memories of the past behind, blocking out what she hadn't been able to control, and focusing on the present. She was here now, and this girl needed her.

End of story.

Haanes Westergaard spoke loudly, and Emma jumped. She hadn't even known he was close enough to hear their conversation. "I know Ford Clark is behind this. He's jealous because Astrid is earning better points in the ski races than his daughter Mandy." Haanes took a step toward Ford, thrusting his finger in the man's direction. "He's trying to take out Mandy's competition, so she'll make the Olympic team."

"I am doing no such thing," Ford Clark roared, surging to his feet from a nearby table. He was a short, stocky man with a bald head and a black beard. "I'm an honorable man. We don't do things like that around here. *You're* the questionable outsider." He clenched his fists. "I can't help it your daughter isn't good enough to make it in the European academies. You know that's why you used your connections to get her enrolled in Coldwater Cove Ski Academy." Ford took a step toward Haanes, thrusting his finger right back. "She doesn't belong here anymore than you do."

Mandy started to cry at the table beside her mother, Betty. Betty glared at the men and then softened her gaze as it landed on Haanes' wife, Carina, who sat in a silent state of shock, dabbing her own eyes. Betty was homecooked meals and simple pleasures while Carina was Michelin star restaurants and sophisticated tastes, but at the end of the day, they were both mothers.

"Gentlemen, we're wasting time and this is getting us nowhere." Trent stepped between the men, and Gunner strategically placed himself off to the side, looking ready to have the sheriff's back if necessary.

The men returned to their tables without another word.

The door to the community center opened on a gust of wind and a flurry of snow. Emma's parents and Jack hurried inside, quickly closing the door behind them. They dusted their coats off and looked around the room. Finally spotting her, they rushed to her side and hugged her for a long moment.

"Are you okay, honey?" her mother asked.

"How's your arm, Bean?" her father asked simultaneously.

"I'm okay." She blew out a shaky breath. "Getting shot at was worse than the bullet grazing my arm. I don't ever want to feel that vulnerable again." Her eyes met Gunner's. "I can't even think about what might have happened if this guy hadn't been doing something as foolish as ice fishing when he knew a nor'easter was headed our way."

"They would have finished you off, or you would have frozen to death on the ice. That's what would have happened," he said matter of fact. His hazel gaze locked hers in place. "Guess my being foolish was your lucky day."

"Seems to me chasing storms is foolish," Jack chimed in, then grunted as he glanced at her arm.

"Storm chasing isn't foolish." Emma studied Jack, wishing he would understand why she did what she did. He looked so much like her, but he didn't have the same connection as... "It's necessary," she blurted. "At least I'm trying to make a difference."

Emma shot a glare at Gunner. She was thankful to him and had told him as much, but there was something about him that got under her skin.

Ignoring both him and her brother, she turned to her parents. "Dr. Jeffries said I'll be fine and bandaged my arm. It's just a flesh wound. I didn't know Dr. Hurn retired."

"She married Stacy's father, Mack Buchannan, and they're enjoying their retirement by sailing to all sorts of places on their bucket list," Emma's father, Ben, said.

Her mother, Dori, smiled with stars in her eyes. "Isn't it romantic?"

Her brother, Jack, scowled. "There's a lot of things that have changed since you've been gone." He stuffed his hands in his pockets, drawing her attention once more. "You're not the only one hurting, Em." He clenched his jaw, and a muscle bulged as his Adam's apple bobbed once.

Emma couldn't take the tension between them anymore. She threw herself against him and hugged him the best she could with a bandaged arm, holding back her tears. She hadn't cried over what had happened because she knew if she did, she would never stop. "I'm sorry," she whispered.

After a moment's hesitation, his strong arms wrapped around her and held on as if they would never let her go. "I'm just glad you're here now." He leaned back, glancing down at her bandage. "Don't ever scare me like that again. I can't lose you, too."

She nodded but couldn't speak past the lump in her throat.

"Dori. Ben." Sheriff West nodded as he rejoined them with Stacy by his side. "Glad to see you're all okay. How are the roads, Jack?"

"Terrible. The marina's a mess. The Claw survived the surge, barely, but the entire town sustained a lot of damage and the storm's not even done yet." Jack shook his head. "My guys are out plowing, doing the best they can, but even they can't keep up with the snow. It's dangerous out there. We brought the sleds here to see if you needed help."

"Much appreciated. We need everyone who is physically able to chip in. It's a community effort at a time like this. We have reports of several vehicles off roads with stranded motorists that some of my deputies are handling, while the others are rescuing homeowners in need."

"I heard the governor issued a state of emergency with a travel ban."

"Yeah, a little too late, and this town is too stubborn to heed the National Weather Service's warning to evacuate, making my job far more difficult. I only stopped into the community center to check on things here. As long as Bart can keep our generator going, we won't freeze to death and our supplies won't spoil." Trent looked at Stacy. "Where are we at with everything else?"

"Well, Laura asked Coach Randall and Coach Hall to come to the center to help distract the athletes from the academy as well as the local high school kids. She also asked Vanessa Taylor to bring her salon supplies to cheer everyone up, and Harry Smith brought over a variety of desserts from the diner. The school board president, Mark Jessup, is here along with town council president, Kimberly Caldwell, to donate games and art supplies. The storm hit earlier than we expected, but most of our preparations were already in place."

Stacy clarified to Emma and Gunner that Laura Flemming was her best friend, who had been elected as mayor a while back. Laura used to be the county clerk but after the last mayor and the sheriff were both arrested for corruption, Laura was elected the new mayor and Stacy's husband, Trent, was elected the new sheriff. The three of them worked closely together in Stacy's late mother's honor to make Coldwater Cove a better place.

Laura had her hands full these days. The coaches were always at odds, fighting over which school the young athletes would attend. Serious athletes attended the academy on the outskirts of town, skiing all day on their own private hill and going to school at night, staying right on campus in the dorms. The local high school coach was just trying to keep his ski team competitive, but everyone knew that if you had dreams of the Olympics, you attended the academy.

Then there was the matter of the school board and the town council. Even back when Emma lived in Coldwater Cove, there had always been ongoing arguments on how the town's money should be spent. This time was no different. Apparently, Mark wanted more money for athletics while Kimberly wanted more funds for the arts. As mayor, it was Laura's job to allocate the funds as she saw fit. No mayor could keep everyone happy, but Laura was doing her best.

Jack's phone suddenly went off. "Ross here, what's up?" He listened, his face growing grave as he met the sheriff's eyes. "Thanks for letting me know, but don't do anything. I'll take care of it. We don't need you trapped, too. "On top of everything else, Jack was also a volunteer firefighter.

"What's wrong?" Trent asked.

"Ester Wilson's roof just caved in. My plow guy, Travis, lives across the street. He has a generator, so he went home after we shut the plows down. Ester does not. He was going to see if he could get inside, but I told him not to. The snow has been falling at two inches per hour. The rest of that roof could go at any minute."

"You know how to drive a sled?" Trent asked Gunner.

Gunner nodded once.

"Good. The three of us will head out. At Ester's age, every minute counts."

Emma couldn't help but think that when bullets and blizzards were involved, every minute counted at *any* age. She silently vowed, *Hang in there, Astrid. I'm coming. I won't leave you alone. Not this time.*

4

HARVEY PUSHED his glasses up his nose and dialed Emma's cell phone for the tenth time but didn't get through. He'd been trying her phone all day with no luck. He took a sip of coffee and turned up the nightly news while he paced the open floor plan kitchen and living room in his bare feet. He wore the soft cotton gray checkered sleep pants and t-shirt set Emma had bought him this past Christmas.

"Why did we let her go alone?" he said out loud to himself.

The nor'easter had struck Coldwater Cove hard according to the National Weather Bureau. The news had reported the storm had torn up the harbor then moved inland and had already dumped a foot of snow. The town had lost power and the roads were closed, leaving no way in or out until the storm cleared.

"Still no word?" JoJo asked as she came out of her bedroom in the three-bedroom townhouse they all shared in Norfolk, Virginia. The three of them were on the road so much and all single. It made sense to stay in one place and share the bills.

JoJo wore Tweety Bird flannel pajamas and fuzzy slippers, with her pink hair sticking out in twenty di-

33

rections. She didn't have a stitch of makeup on, yet she was about the prettiest thing he'd ever seen. She tried so hard to act like a badass, but underneath her tough exterior, she was a softie.

"No. She's not answering her phone." He looked at JoJo, not hiding anything he was feeling from his face.

"I'm worried, too." She touched his forearm, her pale fingers warm against his dark skin, the contrast doing funny things to his insides.

He stepped away and paced. JoJo was a firecracker. He'd always been attracted to her, but her brother was one of his best friends. Besides, they worked together. He knew enough people who had formed a romantic relationship with a coworker to know it rarely ended well. Bad vibes between any of them was the last thing their team needed.

"How's The Beast coming along?" he asked, pouring her a cup of black coffee.

"Thanks." She took a hearty sip and hummed. "She's coming along. I still have a few things I want to tweak on her, but for the most part, she's ready to roll. Any updates on the storm? What do the meteorologists have to say?"

"According to the Miller Classification, they determined the nor'easter to be a Type A." He puckered his brow. "That's not good."

"English, Harv. Speak English. You and Em are the college grads, remember? I just drive The Beast, and a nor'easter isn't the type of storm we usually chase."

"The Miller classification system is used to determine the track and severity of a nor'easter. Storms are classified into two categories. Type A storms form in the Gulf of Mexico, the Carolinas, and Georgia. They cause heavy snow by the time they reach New England. While Type B storms are caused from a low-pressure system over the Ohio Valley that..." He used his hands to create a visual as JoJo's eyes glassed over. "Reforms, if you will, onto the Gulf Stream. These storms bring winter-like precipitation from the Great Plains and the Ohio River Valley to the Southeast." He paused until he had her attention. "The nor'easter in Coldwater Cove is a Type A storm."

"Kind of like you. Type A and complicated." She grunted. "Why can't you just say the weathermen say it's a big storm that's dropping lots of snow? Why does everything have to be so formal and complicated with you?" She sipped her coffee, staring at him with her lavender eyes over the rim.

"Fine. Big storm. Lots of snow. No power. Roads closed. Radio silent Emma." He stared right back at JoJo. "Better?"

"Much." She grinned. "What's the plan?"

"I was hoping you would tell me."

"Finally. Now you're starting to make sense. You stick with me, kid, and you'll be all right."

"Okay," he said.

She blinked. "Okay?"

"Nothing complicated about that." He fought a smile.

For the first time since he'd known JoJo Coletrain, she was speechless. Maybe there was something to be said about simplicity after all.

* * *

THE SNOW WAS STILL COMING DOWN heavy, but the wind had let up enough, improving the visibility to where Emma and Gunner could make their way back to the hotel down the street. It had been a long day: getting shot, then snowed in by a blizzard, and then helping everyone in the community center while Gunner, Jack, and the sheriff rescued Ester after her roof caved in.

For hours, they rescued several other stranded people as well. It was late, and everyone was cold and tired. Jack told Gunner to take a sled, and Emma rode on the back.

They pulled into the parking lot of the hotel and parked right by a side door under an overhang to semi-protect the snowmobile from the elements as much as they could. Emma climbed off the back of the sled and used her room key to open the hotel door, holding it open for Gunner who was right behind her. They walked down the hall in silence until they reached their rooms.

"Gunner?" Emma said softly when he opened the door to his room.

He paused but didn't say anything. He just looked at her over his shoulder with those mesmerizing hazel eyes of his.

"Would you like to come in for a drink? I mean, you don't have to, but if you want to you could." She pressed her lips together. Whenever she was nervous, she rambled.

He arched a brow.

She inhaled deep, then said in a calmer tone, "I have some beer, and well, I really don't want to be alone. I may look like I'm fine but getting shot really freaked me out. I think the reality of what happened to me is finally settling in."

He slowly closed his door and nodded.

Turning around before he could change his mind, she opened her door and led the way inside. She barely knew the man, but he'd saved her life. She felt safe with him, and right now, that's what she needed.

She stripped off her hat, coat, and boots then headed straight to her minifridge and pulled out two longnecks. Popping the tops off both, she carried the beers to the center of the room and stopped short. Suddenly all she could see was the big king-sized bed.

Memories of thinking about an affair whispered through her mind.

Her cheeks flooded with heat. She was horrible when it came to romance and dating. That was why she pretty much avoided the whole thing, but sex was a means to an end. Nature's way of reducing tension and making a person forget about their worries, no strings attached.

"You okay?" a deep voice said, snapping her back to reality. "You look flushed." He'd taken off his outer wear as well.

She shook her head hard to rid her brain of those dangerous thoughts, praying he hadn't read her mind, and handed him a beer. He'd chosen the chair in the corner, thank God, but it was still close enough that she could smell his scent. She cleared her throat and sat on the chair in front of the desk, smiling a little too big.

"Just tired," she said truthfully.

"Roger that." He took a long drink of his beer.

She couldn't look away from his Adam's apple bobbing as he swallowed. He finally lowered his beer, bless the Lord, but then he ran a hand over his military haircut and down the back of his neck, which was even sexier. She stared at his full lips. Maybe she should just sleep with him and get it over with. It would certainly relieve the stress she was feeling.

"No."

She blinked. "No what?"

"Yes, I've thought about sleeping with you from the second I first laid eyes on you, but no we shouldn't give in to our desires."

Holy crap, he could read her mind. "W-We shouldn't?" She swallowed hard. Hearing him voice her thoughts out loud in that sexy deep voice of his that strummed the chords in her belly like a bass guitar unnerved her.

"You're only here temporarily, and so am I," he said logically.

She met his gaze, which was now hooded, but heat still blazed through the slits. "Isn't that the point?" she said in a voice even she didn't recognize.

"Normally, yes." His gaze focused on *her* lips this time, until he finally lifted his eyes to lock on hers. "You've been shot. Your body can only handle so much in one day. The adrenaline that's kept you going all day is about to wear off, and you're going to crash. This town is in the middle of a natural disaster, attempted murderers are still on the loose, and a teenage girl is missing. If we're going to be of any help, we need to stay focused. Our personal needs don't matter."

"Right...focused," she managed to get out, but all she could *focus* on was that Greek god body of his. Maybe she'd hit her head on the ice because, clearly, she wasn't thinking straight. All she knew for certain was that exhaustion was setting in quickly, and the beer had gone straight to her head.

His lips twitched with the hint of a smile. "Go to bed."

"Uh-huh." She nodded, still staring at his impressive pecs clearly visible through his shirt. Slowly blinking, she could barely keep her eyes open. Damn, why'd he have to be right about everything? The adrenaline rush had finally dissipated, and she was crashing hard.

"Right." He finished his beer and set his bottle down, then slowly stood and walked over to her.

She felt him scoop her up into his arms. "Wh-What are you doing?"

"Taking you to bed, sweetheart," he whispered in her ear as he laid her on the mattress, and her eyes closed immediately. She felt him pull the covers over her and kiss the top of her head, then she drifted into the deepest sleep she'd had in a very long time.

* * *

"WHAT THE HELL are you doing, Nash?" Gunner said to himself as he stared down at the blond bombshell on the bed before him.

Emma really had no idea what a knockout she was. She had a natural beauty, where she didn't even have to try to look sexy. She brought out protective feelings inside of him, and that was the last thing he needed. He couldn't afford to feel protective toward anyone because it hurt too much when you failed to protect them and let them down.

He scrubbed his hands over his face, feeling the whiskers. He needed a shave and a haircut. It wasn't like him not to be perfectly put together and in control. His lips turned down. Then again, nothing about him had been the same since his last deployment. What the hell had he gotten himself into? The storm he could handle, but people getting shot hit too close to home for comfort.

He couldn't do this again.

He never should have gone into her room for a beer, he thought as he headed for the door. Glancing over his shoulder one last time to be sure she was safely tucked into bed, he let himself out, locking the door behind him and checking it twice. He headed into his own room, thinking about the shooting and the missing girl.

Those men were no amateurs.

They knew how to handle a gun. Their stance, the way they dropped to a knee, and the fact that they didn't miss at that distance indicated some sort of sniper training. Ex-military or law enforcement maybe. What did they want with an international athlete at the top of her game? A rising ski star with several endorsements under her belt already?

He thought about that for a minute. Was it a competition thing like her father had suggested? Or may be an enemy of her wealthy father, looking to blackmail him and cash in on his famous daughter? In Gunner's line of work, he might be the muscle, but he had connections as well.

Maybe it was time he called in a few favors of his own.

* * *

EMMA WOKE up the next morning feeling as if she hadn't slept a wink. She'd crashed hard, but then she'd tossed and turned all night with dreams of one incredibly hot Navy Seal. She groaned. How embarrassing. She'd practically thrown herself at him, and he'd shot her down. He clearly wasn't interested, which was a good thing, she reminded herself.

For a while yesterday they didn't have cell service, and when it finally came back on, her phone had died. She'd charged it overnight. Turning it on, she checked messages. Oh, boy. Harvey wasn't going to be happy with her. She'd missed a dozen calls from him yesterday. Dialing his number, he picked up on the first ring.

"Thank God you're alive," Harvey's voice boomed through the phone.

"I've been better, but I'll live."

There was a pause on the line. "What the hell does that mean?"

"There's a teenage girl missing. She was kidnapped, and I was shot."

"What? I knew we should have gone with you," JoJo's voice raised an octave. He obviously had Emma on speaker phone. "Give me that phone." There was the sound of a scuffle. "How do you get shot during a nor'easter?" JoJo finally asked.

"That's what I'm trying to figure out."

"Em, don't do anything to put yourself in any more danger." Harvey took control of the phone once more. "What happened anyway?"

Emma explained everything that happened, without having to agree to keep herself out of danger. She didn't want to have to lie to her friends, but she would do just about anything to rescue that girl.

"The weather shows you guys are still getting hammered with snow. They won't be going anywhere until the weather clears, if they're even alive."

"That's the point." Emma closed her eyes in frustration. No one seemed to understand the gravity of the situation. "The minute the storm clears, we'll only have a day or two before they disappear with her for good. I can't let that happen."

"Well, you can't do this alone," JoJo piped in from the background.

"I'm not alone. There's a Navy Seal in town who's agreed to help me." He hadn't yet, but it was only a matter of time before he would. Protecting and rescuing people was in his blood. Emma was banking on that.

She hung up after reassuring her friends she wouldn't do anything on her own. She knew storms, and Gunner knew survival. Together, they were the only chance Astrid Westergaard had. Emma quickly changed and grabbed her backpack, planning to head back over to the community center. She checked her pack to make sure she had everything she needed when she noticed a folded-up piece of paper.

She frowned. She didn't remember putting any notes in her pack. Unfolding the paper, she blinked and her mouth fell open. The note was typed on standard typing paper, so there was no way to trace who might have written it, but the message was clear.

BACK OFF, BITCH! STOP STICKING YOUR NOSE IN PLACES IT DOESN'T BELONG, OR NEXT TIME I'll SHOOT TO KILL! SHOW ANYONE THIS NOTE, AND THE GIRL DIES!

EMMA'S HANDS shook so hard, the note fluttered to the floor. There was no way those men had made it back to town in that storm to put the note in her pack. They had to be out in the woods still. Her eyes darted wildly around her room. It didn't look tampered with, so that meant only one thing. Someone inside the community center was a mole. A mole who was clever. A mole who was dangerous….

A mole who knew where that girl was.

5

<hr>

"Obviously the pressure is too much for these girls. For all we know, Astrid may have willingly run away with those men," Coach Hall said, wearing jeans and a sweatshirt with a ball cap over his jet-black hair. "If any of these girls want to switch to the high school's ski team, you have no say in the matter."

"Look, I get it. You're trying to have a competitive season and to do that, you need good skiers. But a high school team doesn't come close to an Olympic team. Clearly, you've lost your mind," Coach Randall replied, wearing a warm-up suit with the team's logo, his deep auburn hair perfectly styled. "Astrid is at the top of her game. There's no way she would have run away from all that. You know these girls stand the best chance of making the Olympic team by sticking with the academy."

"Gentlemen, this is not the time or the place," Stacy said, giving them both a meaningful look. "Harry just brought in more desserts. Why don't you have each of your teams get some before everyone polishes them off." They didn't say another word to each other but left to do her bidding.

"The girls do look a little shook up," Emma said as she joined Stacy, having heard the whole conversation.

Gunner had given her a ride back to the community center this morning on the sled. Neither of them had mentioned the night before, and she certainly hadn't mentioned the note she'd found. She couldn't help studying everyone in the room or avoiding Gunner. There were more important matters to worry about than her wounded ego.

"I'll give them all manicures," a woman said from the table right behind them. She stood up, wearing a knockout dress and heels that made her already tall height even taller, and grabbed the handle of her suitcase on wheels full of supplies from a salon.

"Thank you, Vanessa. You've been a big distraction for these girls." Stacy smiled. "We all really appreciate it."

"Who doesn't love to be pampered with hair, makeup, and nail makeovers?" Vanessa winked. "These poor girls have such busy schedules, they never have time for self-care, but don't you worry. I've got them covered." She walked toward the group of girls with a bright smile on her face.

"Wow, she's stunning," Emma said. The woman had waist length, thick black hair, creamy pale skin, and eyes such a light blue they almost looked clear. Not to mention her body looked like a runway model's.

"Yes, she is. She was a former Miss USA. She put Coldwater Cove on the map as the only famous person to come from our small town. She traveled around a bit, then came back here to share her knowledge of all things beauty with the locals by opening her own salon. From what I can tell, she's done very well for herself."

"I can relate to those young athletes. Storm chasing is so demanding, I never have time for self-care." Emma glanced at her pathetic fingernails, then pulled the sleeves of her sweater down over her hands. Not that she ever had anyone to get dolled up for. Her gaze was drawn to the stage where Gunner was talking to Jack and the sheriff.

"Maybe you'll get the chance while you're here. I've used her myself. She's very talented." Stacy's gaze followed Emma's. "Trent loves it when I put in the effort. Most men do." Her eyes held a twinkle.

"Well, I wouldn't know much about that," Emma said, then cleared her throat. "So, Jack said you wanted to talk to me?"

"Yes." Stacy flipped through her notes, her facial expression turning her into the serious journalist she was. "I wanted to go over one more time exactly what happened out on that ice. Any details at all that come to mind about that day might help us to figure out who is behind the shooting and why."

"Okay, I'll try."

"I mean, if they were kidnappers, you would think they would have reached out to Astrid's father already. Then again, the storm is most likely an issue for them, I'm sure. If the men are trying to take out the competition like Astrid's father thinks, then it's likely he wouldn't hear from them at all. If Astrid ran away on her own because of the stress like the coach thinks, then it's also likely her father wouldn't hear from them. So, anything at all you can tell me, just might be a game changer."

Emma's gaze scanned the community center, still full of half the town. Ford was whispering to some other local academy fathers while giving Haanes dirty looks. Kimberly Caldwell was in a heated argument with Mark Jessup over his athletic supplies taking up too much room for her to set up her art supplies. Harry was scolding the maintenance man, Bart, for eating half the pan of cinnamon rolls.

Tensions were running high.

The mole could be anyone. They could be watching her right now and get word to the men to kill Astrid if they suspected Emma said anything to Stacy or the Sheriff. Emma's heart began to pound and her palms started sweating. What if she was putting the girl in more danger just by being at the community center?

"Emma? Are you okay?" Stacy brought Emma's attention back to her.

"Sorry. Yes, I'm fine. Just a little tired. I didn't get much sleep last night."

"That's understandable. You've been through a lot." Stacy closed her notebook. "Why don't you think on it and let me know if anything comes to mind." She looked across the room. "I'm going to catch up with Laura to see about bringing in more food. We can't live off of just desserts, and it looks as if most of those are gone anyway."

"Thanks, Stacy." Emma watched her leave and noticed her parents talking to her brother. She headed in their direction.

A feeling of being watched settled over her again. She turned around in a full circle but didn't see anything. She felt like she was losing her mind. Someone wanted to keep her silent, and she needed to find out who before they made her disappear as well.

* * *

GUNNER WATCHED Emma walk over to her parents and brother. She hadn't said a word about last night, so he'd taken his cue from her. Maybe she didn't even remember it, which would be okay with him. He'd come dangerously close to taking her up on her offer last night, but that would have been a big mistake.

She didn't need damaged goods like him.

There was something about her that drew him to her in a way that he hadn't experienced before. He'd been with plenty of women to satisfy a basic human need, but he hadn't ever let his guard down. He didn't like being vulnerable. His focus had always been on being the best soldier he could be and making a difference in the world. He didn't have time for foolish games of the heart and certainly couldn't afford to get distracted.

Up until now, it had been easy for him to keep his priorities straight and focus on the mission at hand. But Emma was different. He couldn't stop thinking about her. She was spunky and driven and amused the hell out of him without even trying. She had no idea of her appeal, and that was somehow far more dangerous.

So as soon as they'd entered the community center, he'd made a beeline for Trent and Jack to check in. Out of sight, out of mind. At least that was what he was hoping for. The storm was still raging outside, so any rescue attempts for the girl were still out of the question. But that didn't mean the sheriff wasn't trying to figure out who the men were with the girl, and why they wanted her.

Gunner sighed. Who was he kidding? He couldn't avoid Emma forever.

His gaze had been drawn to her all morning and he could feel her presence without even looking at her. Avoiding her was childish, and he wasn't a child. He started walking in her direction when he saw a movement behind the curtains by the stage.

There were a lot of people still staying in the community center, but hiding behind a curtain just felt sneaky. Gunner's radar went on high alert. He made his way toward the stage then moved close enough to the curtain without looking suspicious. He bent down to tie his shoe and could hear someone talking.

It was only one voice, as if the person were on a cell phone. They were talking with a hushed tone that was difficult to make out and pausing in between to listen. Gunner stood up and grabbed an orange from a fruit bowl on the stage. He leaned against the wood and slowly started to peel the orange to buy himself time as he strained to hear the words being said.

"You told me we wouldn't get caught." The voice sounded panicked.

A heavy pause hung in the air.

"I'm telling you; I'm not going down for this alone," the person hissed, the tone still hushed and unrecognizable.

Another lengthy pause happened.

"This wasn't part of the deal," the person growled. "If this comes back to ruin me, I have connections."

Another pause.

"Someone's coming. I have to go."

"What the hell are you doing back here, being all sneaky?" a different voice demanded in an angry tone, hushed like the first one had been.

"None of your damn business," the first voice growled just as angry.

"Like hell it isn't."

"Yeah? What are you gonna do about it?"

Gunner rolled the orange beneath the curtain and followed it.

Clark Ford and Haanes Westergaard stood there with raised fists and red faces, looking at him in surprise.

"Whoops, sorry, fellas." He picked up the orange and tossed it in the air to catch it. "Slippery little thing."

Haanes straightened his jacket, speaking with a normal tone now. "I was looking for something myself." His gaze hardened on Clark. "Unfortunately, I didn't find what I was looking for."

Clark narrowed his eyes, his voice full volume as well, sounding vastly different from the hushed whispers. "Me neither, but don't worry. I will eventually." He turned around and left without another word.

Haanes clenched his jaw, then nodded once at Gunner before leaving in the other direction.

Both men looked guilty of something, but what? The bigger question was which one of them had been the voice on the phone...?

And who was on the other end of the line?

* * *

JACK STOOD there listening to his sister Emma talk to his parents. He was still angry with her for not coming home sooner. She hadn't been home since she graduated from college. It had been five years. Five years of missed holidays. Five years of missed birthdays.

Five years of excuses.

He knew coming home meant facing her demons and all the painful memories that went along with that, but that didn't mean staying away was okay. It wasn't. His parents missed her terribly, and admittedly, so did he. She put herself in danger all the time with the career path she'd chosen. Jack knew the nor'easter was what had finally brought her home again. And now she wanted to run off into the woods in the middle of a blizzard.

That was the dumbest, most reckless and insensitive thing to do, especially after what had happened.

"Em, we get it. We all know exactly how you feel about leaving a defenseless teenager out in the storm. We really do, but it's not safe. We need all the sleds we have and the manpower to go with it just to rescue the people in town. We can't risk venturing into the woods. There's no visibility out there, and there's no cell service the deeper you go. You need to be reasonable about this."

"I would expect that from the sheriff, but not from you." She stared at him, her green eyes shimmering with unshed tears and burning a hole straight to his heart. "I thought you above anyone would understand and be on my side."

"We just can't risk losing you, too, honey." Their mother hugged Emma, rocking her back and forth.

"The moment this storm is over with, we'll be there right by your side in searching for her." Their father patted her back.

Emma stepped away from them. "Don't you see? The minute the storm clears, we'll never see the poor girl again. No one will. If we have any chance at all of reaching her in time, it has to be while the storm is still happening. I know storms, and Gunner is a Navy Seal. He knows survival. How can we not take advantage of that? We're her only hope. If we don't act now, it will be too late."

"Whoa, I never agreed to a search and rescue mission," Gunner said while holding his hands up before him as he joined them. "Sorry, Ms. Ross, but I have to agree with your family. Those two men don't deserve to be saved, and there's only one girl. The risk of losing several people isn't worth the reward of saving one girl. Surely you can see the logic, given the scenario."

Jack really liked Gunner. He didn't say a lot, but what he said had merit. He seemed to be a man of honor and integrity, even if he did harbor a few demons of his own. He hadn't confided in what they were, but Jack had been a bartender long enough to recognize when someone was troubled.

"I see no such thing." She hoisted her chin a notch. "The only thing I see is a bunch of people who are too afraid to take a chance."

"I'm not afraid. I'm rational," Gunner said, remaining calm without giving anything he was feeling away by his neutral expression. "You're clearly not."

She gasped, looking about to object further, when the front door to the community center flew open.

"What the hell?" Jack gaped. "Who the hell is that?"

In walked a man almost as tall and big as Gunner, wearing a bright white parka that made him look twice as large. All you could see from beneath his hood were a pair of glasses looking out at them.

Jack peered beyond him, and his eyes widened further as he muttered, "And *what* the hell is that?"

A woman emerged from behind him to take the lead. She was half his size but clearly the one in charge. She wore a bright pink one piece snowsuit that was skintight. She didn't wear a hood over her bright pink hair that stuck out in several directions. She wore pink fuzzy earmuffs the same color as the enormous bubble she just blew.

Emma squealed and ran in their direction, throwing herself into their arms to hug them both at the same time.

"I take it she knows them?" Gunner asked.

"My guess is that would be what she calls her Dream Team." Jack shook his head, his stomach filling with acid and giving him heartburn. From all that he'd heard, they were nearly as reckless as his sister was. His sister didn't need anyone on her side who might just take her up on her plea of being foolish.

"Dream Team? As in storm chasing team?" Gunner looked as worried as Jack felt. "What do you think they're doing here?"

"I don't know, but I do know their timing couldn't be worse."

6

WHAT THE HELL are they doing here?

The Michelin Tire Man and pink flamingo next to him nearly ran me over when they barged through the front door of the community center, bringing a flurry of snow inside with them. The town was in a state of emergency. How the hell had they gotten here? And why would they come? It didn't make any sense.

Who *willingly* drove into a nor'easter?

My stomach twisted into knots. I wouldn't be surprised if I had an ulcer. I'd never been one to handle stress well. My life would be a whole lot easier if Emma Ross would do as she was fucking told. The meddling woman did *not* need anyone on her side willing to help her look for the girl. It was bad enough she had the giant watching over her every move. It had been really hard to sneak the note into her backpack. That man was always on alert. Always looking around the community center....

Always paying attention.

The two incompetent thugs I'd hired had finally called me from the HAM radio I'd given them once they'd reached the first cabin. Before they'd taken the girl, I'd given them directions to a few different cabins the locals owned. I knew they would be fully stocked for emergencies such as this. I didn't want any evidence left behind on the identity of my guys, so I'd specifically told them the cabin was only to be used as a last resort, in case things went to hell in a hand basket.

A blizzard was going about as far into hell as you could get.

I'd heard the Navy Seal say he'd shot one of the men, but I hadn't realized how bad the situation was. My man confirmed he'd lost a lot of blood, but they'd found supplies to patch his wound until the storm blew over. There was no way they could leave before then. The girl was fine, and so was my other man. They had enough food to get by for a few more days, and they still had their weapons.

The plan was that as soon as the weather cleared, the men would get out of town and would finish our agreement. Everything depended on this deal going through as planned. I'd worked my ass off to get where I was today. I deserved to be rewarded. I wasn't about to let some meddling bitch fuck up my future.

Emma called the newcomers her Dream Team, pulling me from my troubled thoughts. I listened to them confirm the roads were still closed and there was still a state of emergency with no unnecessary travel, but they had managed to drive through the storm in a vehicle called The Beast. It sounded more like an armored tank built to withstand anything mother nature threw at her.

The pink flamingo was a spitfire. Definitely the one in charge over the tire man, who seemed to be more of a lapdog than a guard dog. I tightened my jaw and ground my teeth, making my temples throb. If Emma convinced them to look for the girl before the storm let up, I would be forced to have my guys kill the girl and abandon the plan.

Dammit!

I couldn't let that happen. I had to do something. I needed to up my game in scaring Emma into behaving before it was too late. I wasn't a killer, but there was a first time for everything.

And right about now I had murder on the brain.

* * *

"I can't believe you guys are here," Emma said to Harvey and JoJo.

They sat at a table with her parents, brother, and Gunner after introducing them to her Dream Team. She should have known they would find a way to come to her in her time of need. They'd never let her down before. This time shouldn't be any different. Although, she did feel guilty about cutting their R&R short.

"I have to admit I had my doubts, but JoJo insisted The Beast was ready." Harvey pushed his glasses up his nose, then warmed his hands on his mug as he blew into his hot chocolate before taking a sip.

"You questioning my mechanical skills, Harv?" JoJo squinted at him, scrubbing a hand through her short, cropped pink hair.

"I would never." His face looked serious.

"See that you don't." She tipped her head, then chugged her black coffee.

"However you got here, we're glad you made it." Jack let out a big breath. "We can definitely use the help."

"You got it." Harvey nodded.

"Don't take this wrong, but why are you here?" Emma's father asked. He nursed a cup of coffee and eyed the Dynamic Duo curiously.

"Are you kidding? Astrid Westergaard's disappearance is all over the news." JoJo looked at Emma's bandaged arm. "And your headstrong daughter obviously needs someone to keep her out of danger."

Emma gasped. "Hey!"

"That's what I've been trying to tell her." Jack looked at Emma. "I like this one." He pointed at JoJo.

Harvey frowned.

JoJo grinned.

Emma raised her brows.

What the heck was going on with her Dream Team? She shook her head. "Don't worry about me. I can take care of myself."

"Can you?" Gunner asked quietly.

All eyes zeroed in on him. For a moment, he looked like he regretted speaking, but then his face transformed into his usual unreadable mask.

"Yes, Mr. Nash, I can." Emma stared him down for a moment.

The man had shot her down the night before then ignored her all day today. If he hadn't wanted to sleep with her, that was fine, but he didn't have to act like she had some disease the next day.

"I'm grateful for your help thus far, but you don't have to concern yourself about me anymore." Emma stood and looked at her friends. "I'll grab you guys some food, then I want to talk to you about something."

"Here we go again," Jack mumbled under his breath, but Emma heard him.

"I'll help you, dear." Her mother jumped up between them and took her arm before she had a chance to say what was really on her mind.

"Thanks, Mom." Emma finally spoke when they were far enough away from the table and over by the stage where the food was set up. She grabbed a plate and started filling it more forcefully than she'd intended.

Her mother did the same with a lot more care. "You

know your brother loves you. He's just worried. We're all a little worried," she admitted, keeping her eyes on the plates. "Sometimes you don't think before you act. Your impulsiveness might be exciting for you, but it's terrifying for the rest of us."

"I know." Emma touched her mother's arm until she stopped moving and looked at her. "I hate that I worry you, but sometimes I can't help myself. Chasing a storm is when I feel the closest to her."

Her mother squeezed her hand. "I understand how you feel. I can't look at a storm without thinking of her, but if we lost you too, I don't know how we would get through that. Please be careful." She kissed her cheek. "For me."

"Okay." Emma hadn't really thought about how her actions affected her family. All she knew was she had a burning desire to feel the power of a storm. Feel what it was like to be in the middle of one.

Feel what Ellie must have felt.

"Honey, can you get more rolls? They're in the storage room in the back. I'll take these plates over to your friends. I really like them by the way."

Emma smiled. "I do too. See you back at the table in five." She watched her mother walk away with the food, then she headed in the back to get the rolls.

Entering the storage room, she turned on the light and looked around. Rows of shelves lined the walls with supplies on them. The center of the room had free standing shelves as well, reminding her of a library. Wandering up and down each row, looking for the rolls, the lights suddenly shut off. She jumped and stopped moving, her stomach flipping over. A tingly sensation swept over her.

"Hello? Is anyone there?" Emma asked.

Silence.

She waited another beat but didn't hear anything.

Huh. That was weird. Maybe there was something wrong with the generator. She'd have to tell the maintenance man, Bart, as soon as she found her way out. The storage room didn't have any windows, so it was pitch black inside. She started feeling her way towards what she thought might be the door, but it was hard to tell. She was disoriented with it being so dark.

A noise whispered softly through the room.

The hairs stood up all over her body and goosebumps peppered her flesh. "Hello?"

Silence.

Was she imagining things? Shaking her head, she kept moving. Another noise sounded, this time a little louder. A shuffle. Almost like footsteps. "Look, I know I'm not alone so you can stop playing games."

Silence.

Maybe she really was losing her mind. She'd become paranoid after receiving that note, but there was a room full of people out there. No one would be brazen enough to try something with half the town nearby. She was in the middle of a long row of shelves when suddenly they started falling like dominoes. The shelf in her row got hit and started wobbling. She tried to steady it, but it was too heavy.

Oh, no.

Emma started running, but she wasn't fast enough to clear the row of shelves she was in the middle of. One slammed into her back, knocking her down as it pushed the other shelves over. White hot pain sliced through her skull, and she saw bright white stars behind her eyelids. She felt the blood trickle down her head all the way to her neck. She lay on the floor, feeling the weight of the shelf press down on her. It was getting harder to breathe. She tried to cry out for help, but she couldn't get enough air.

She felt like such a fool.

So much for being able to take care of herself was the last thing to run through her mind before her world went black.

* * *

"WHERE IS EMMA?" Gunner searched the loud, crowded community center.

He thought he'd heard a bang, but it was hard to tell over the pop music being played for the kids. His gut told him something was wrong. Over the years, he'd learned to trust his gut, but after his last mission he questioned everything. Still, the protective side of him urged him to find out for sure.

"Getting rolls from the storage room," her mother replied with a frown. "She should have been back by now. I'll go see if she needs help."

"No, I'll go check on her." Gunner stood, needing to know for himself. "Enjoy your meal."

He made his way across the room, taking note of everyone along the way. He ran into Bart coming out of a maintenance closet. The man looked to be in his fifties, still in decent shape, with a full head of salt and pepper hair. He adjusted his coveralls and locked the door to the closet behind him.

"Have you seen Emma Ross?" Gunner asked.

Bart jumped, then blew out a breath. "I didn't see you there. You scared the crap out of me."

"Sorry." Gunner narrowed his eyes. "Did you?"

Bart's eyes widened. "Did I what? I'm not admitting to anything."

Gunner raised a brow. "See Emma Ross?"

Bart shook his head. "No. Sorry. I gotta go clean up a spill the kids made." He grabbed a mop bucket and headed in a direction that wasn't anywhere near the kids.

This storm was making everyone crazy. Too much togetherness for Gunner's liking. He kept heading toward the storage room. He was just about to pull the door open when out walked Harry Smith, the owner of The Lost Horizon.

"Where's Emma?" Gunner eyed the man suspiciously.

"No clue," Harry said, not quite meeting his eyes. He was a scrawny man with long red hair pulled back in a ponytail and freckles, making him appear younger than he was. No wonder the kids liked him so much. He looked like a kid himself.

"She was last seen in the storage room."

"There's nothing in there but a mess." He held up his camera. "I went in there to set up a makeshift dark room to develop my film, but all the shelves are knocked over. I was just coming out to let Bart know."

Gunner barged past him and called out, "Emma? Emma, where are you? Can you hear me?"

"I told you no one was in there when I went in," Harry said.

A moan sounded from beneath the pile of shelves.

Harry's eyes sprang wide as they met Gunner's. "Look, man, I had nothing to do with that." He held up his hands and backed away.

"Get her brother and the sheriff, now!" Gunner ordered and then sprinted until he reached where the moaning was coming from. "I'm here, Emma. Stay with me."

"Gunner? Is that you?" came a weak muffled voice that sucker punched him in the gut like it always had from the first moment he'd heard it.

"It's me. Can you move?"

"No. My arms and legs are pinned down, and my head hurts like hell, but at least I can breathe."

"Help is on the way."

"Don't leave me." Her voice quivered.

"I'm not going anywhere." He had to stay calm and reassuring.

"The other shelf is holding this one up for now. I never thought I was claustrophobic before, but I'm starting to freak out."

"You're going to be okay. I can relate to claustrophobia. Hell Week was brutal, but I got through it by staying calm and breathing. It's a mental game." He blinked, surprised he'd opened up to her. He never opened up to anyone.

"I've never been a big fan of games."

His lips twitched. "Just keep talking."

"I see light. I'm taking it Bart fixed the generator."

Gunner's smile vanished. "What do you mean?"

"Well, I was in here looking for rolls when the lights went out. That's when the shelves fell over, and I got trapped beneath."

"Emma, the generator never went out."

She paused. "Then how did the lights go off?"

"That's the million-dollar question."

"I'm sure it was just an accident," she said a little too quickly.

"I'm not sure of anything, but you can damn well be sure I'm going to find out."

7

"THANK YOU FOR DOING THIS, VANESSA," Emma said as she sat in a chair while Vanessa Taylor fixed her hair. "I look like a freak."

"I personally like the look." JoJo grinned as she sat in another chair and watched. "Your hair was getting too long anyway."

"It's not so bad," Vanessa said. "You'll still have semi-long hair with chunky new layers. You're lucky they only had to cut a small chunk of your hair off to free you from those shelves." She looked Emma in the eyes with concern. "At least you're still with us. Things could have been much worse." She shuddered, tossing her waist-length hair over her shoulder. "What happened anyway?"

Someone tried to kill me, Emma wanted to say, but she couldn't afford to take that risk. Astrid's life would be in jeopardy if she did. So, she shrugged instead. "I'm such a klutz. It was just a silly accident." Her gaze scanned the room carefully. She'd learned her lesson. The would-be killer was out there watching her.

She could feel it.

Vanessa went back to blending the chunk in with

the other layers, accidentally hitting the bump on the back of Emma's head.

Emma yelped. "Ouch."

"Sorry." Vanessa winced.

"It's okay. Dr. Jeffries said I only have a slight concussion, and you're right, it could have been much worse."

"It took Jack, Harvey, Gunner, and Trent to get you out," JoJo said. "I know you said it was an accident, but the sheriff still put the community center on lockdown while they question everyone just to be sure."

"That's smart. You never can be too careful," Vanessa added. "I've known Jack a long time." She shook her head, her gaze wandering over to him. "I've never seen him so mad. Like mad enough to kill someone over. I pity someone stupid enough to mess with his family. Especially after...you know."

"Yeah," Emma said. "He's very protective."

It was no accident. Someone had definitely tried to kill her, and Emma knew why. It had to be the same person who had put the note in her backpack, warning her to back off or they would have the girl killed. They must have overheard her talking to her family and the Dream Team about wanting to rescue the girl.

Emma needed to be more careful with her words and definitely couldn't tell anyone about the threatening note now. This just confirmed that she needed to do something soon. She was the girl's only hope. The storm was growing weaker. According to her radar, it looked to only have about one more day left.

The time to act was growing near.

"Jack's not the only one who's protective." Vanessa smiled, her words bringing Emma back to the conversation at hand. She followed Vanessa's gaze to find Gunner looking at her. He turned away the second their eyes met, but that didn't stop her from feeling the jolt of electricity that was always between them. "That is one very large, very handsome, very intense man. Half the women in town are smitten with him." Vanessa looked back at Emma and winked. "You're a lucky woman."

"Oh, it's not like that." Emma could feel her cheeks flood with heat.

"Sure, it is." JoJo snorted. "You're just too scared to go for it."

"Not too scared." Emma laughed dryly. "Went for it. Got shot down. Over it now. So, I repeat, it's not like that."

"Then I'd say *he's* the one who's scared," Vanessa said, "because I'm with JoJo. There's no mistaking the way he looks at you."

* * *

GUNNER'S GAZE kept wandering over to Emma while she got her hair cut. Or rather, *fixed*. Every single time she looked at him, his traitorous body reacted. How the hell was he supposed to stay strong and resist her charms when she was on his mind every minute of the day? When he was with her, he couldn't stop looking at her, and when he was away from her, he couldn't stop thinking about her.

That had never happened to him before.

After last night, he'd tried to keep his distance from her all day. But when she'd gone missing, alarm bells rang in his head. Gunner was trained not to panic, especially in the middle of a crisis. All that training went out the window when he'd seen the fallen shelves. Panic had filled his entire body, fearing she was dead.

The way the thought of her demise affected him, told him more than anything else that he was in dangerous waters. He had to admit the sound of her voice, as weak as it was, had been music to his ears. He'd focused and called for help, but it had taken all of them working together to free her.

He would never get the image of her face out of his head. She'd looked so vulnerable when they'd pried the shelves off of her. She'd been pale, bruised, cut, weak, and scared. Her hair had been caught in the hardware of one of the shelves. They'd had to cut a big chunk off to free her.

Gunner cringed at the unmistakable fear in her eyes. He'd seen that same look on his last mission, and had been helpless to save the woman and child. All because someone had lied to him. Someone he'd thought he could trust with his life.

He'd never felt so betrayed.

After that, he'd second guessed everything he knew. If he couldn't trust his gut to tell him when someone was lying, then he couldn't trust anything or anyone. It had messed with his head big time. He'd come to Coldwater Cove to get away and regroup. Yet here he was face-to-face with that same look of terror. Emma claimed the shelves falling on her had been an accident, but his gut said otherwise.

And this time he wasn't going to fail her.

"I've talked to everyone, but no one seems to have seen anything suspicious, and no one appears guilty." Sheriff West ran a hand through his hair, then put his hat back on with a deep and weary sigh.

Gunner liked Trent. He was a former marine and FBI agent, so they related on a lot of things. He knew his frustration. He'd felt it himself many times. Keeping people safe and seeking out justice for wrongs committed took a toll on a person, but people like them didn't concede defeat easily.

"Bart checked the lights in the storage room, and everything seems to be in working order." Jack scrubbed a hand over his face, looking disheveled and stressed out. "How could the lights just go off on their own?"

"Maybe there's a short in the wiring or something," Trent speculated. "When this storm blows over, we'll get a crew in here to fully assess the situation. Until then, we can't hold anyone here who wants to leave without just cause. And unfortunately, we can't prove anything at this point."

"This whole situation feels off. I can't handle anything more happening to my sister. My family can't lose Emma, too, Sheriff."

"They won't, Jack. Not on my watch."

"What do you want me to do, Sheriff?" Gunner asked.

He still had his suspicions and planned to keep his eyes open, but there wasn't much more he could do about it right now.

"Take Emma back to her hotel and keep an eye on her."

"Done." He squared his shoulders.

Protecting people was in his blood. He was through ignoring Emma. He now had a reason to stay close to her. His stomach did a funny little flip, and he frowned. The fact that he was a little too excited about it was a whole different matter.

* * *

"It looks awful, doesn't it?" Emma ran a hand over her layered haircut that fell to her shoulders.

The layers allowed her thick wavy hair to curl more than usual. She wasn't fishing for compliments. She genuinely felt awkward. She'd never liked change. Gunner kept staring at her, and it made her feel self-conscious. Between her foreign hair style and the cuts and bruises to her entire body, she felt like an ugly duckling in front of the man standing in her hotel room doorway looking like a Greek god.

Emma had thrown herself at him once already when she had looked halfway decent, yet he'd shot her down. Now that she looked like a mess, she didn't have high hopes this time. Good Lord could she just crawl under a rock already? This was why she didn't date. Chasing storms was way less scary. She just needed for this day to be over with already.

Gunner's gaze ran over every inch of her entire body, not just her head, and his normally unreadable eyes softened. "I like it. Your hair looks pretty." His eyes locked with hers. "*You* are pretty."

She blinked. "You think so?"

"I know so," he said without hesitation.

Taking a few steps forward, his gaze never left hers as he came to a stop within an inch of her face. She could feel his breath on her mouth, and her lips tingled in anticipation. She licked her lips and couldn't look away.

"You've been through a lot," he said in that deep, sexy voice of his. "You should go to bed."

He had no idea that sleep was the last thing on her mind. She had a promise she planned to fulfill that could put her in danger. The way she figured it, if there was a possibility she could die tomorrow, then she wanted to live today.

"I don't need sleep to get over what I just went through." She stared at his lips, and her breathing grew choppy.

He tried to insist she rest, to no avail. Finally giving in, he made a low, guttural noise deep in his throat then pressed his lips to hers. Slipping his tongue inside, he let it dance sensually over hers and never broke contact as he lifted her to straddle him, kicking the door closed behind him. She moaned and arched her back to get closer to him. He was so big and strong, he easily carried her to the king-sized bed in the middle of the room and laid her on her back, then settled himself between her legs. He started kissing her face and then her neck.

The weight of him on top of her filled her with a moment of panic. Suddenly she was back in the storage room, lying beneath a stack of shelves on top of her, crushing her. She felt like she was going to die all over again. She started breathing in choppy little gasps, feeling like she couldn't get enough air. The room around her faded to black in tunnel vision, and phantom pain sliced through her.

Emma heard a whimper, and it took her a moment to realize it was her own.

Gunner lifted himself up off of her and she sucked in a huge breath of air.

"Emma, talk to me. Are you okay?" His voice was filled with genuine concern.

She took a moment to breathe deeply, over and over, until she returned to normal. She blinked open her eyes and saw the worry on his handsome face. She placed her hand on his rather large chest and bit her bottom lip, taking a moment to compose herself.

"I'm fine," she finally said. "Just a little PTSD from earlier today."

He rolled off of her. "I knew this was a bad idea last night, that's why I walked away. You make me forget my own name. I can't have that. I need to stay alert. And after all you've been through today, this is an even worse idea now." He started to sit up.

"Wait." She quickly rolled on top of him. "You didn't turn me down last night because I repulsed you?"

His hazel eyes widened and then narrowed. "Are you sure your concussion isn't worse? Because you're talking crazy right now." She shifted on top of him, and he closed his eyes tight for a moment, clenching his jaw as if he were counting to ten. He finally opened his eyes and held hers captive. "I have never been so captivated by a woman." He reached up and ran his thumb over her bottom lip. "*Ever.*"

She ran her tongue where his thumb had been, tasting him. Every word he said made her feel warm and fuzzy. "That's not so bad, is it?"

"Yes," he said point blank, sounding troubled. "In my line of work, I can't afford to be distracted."

"But you aren't working right now. Aren't you on R&R?"

"Yeah, but so much for rest and relaxation. The nor'easter I can handle, but kidnappings and shootings and nearly getting crushed to death are not exactly relaxing." He gave her a meaningful look.

"It was just a freak accident. I'm fine. Just a little bruised with a bump on my head." She waved him off.

"PTSD? Clearly, you're not fine." He grunted. "You and I both know that was no accident."

"I don't know what you're talking about." She couldn't quite meet his eyes, and she didn't need him getting more suspicious.

She'd already hinted that she knew storms and he knew survival, so they would make a great rescue team. But he hadn't been interested. He'd made that clear. Neither had her Dream Team. They were all for storm chasing and coming to her aid after she'd been shot, but they had no desire to put themselves in harm's way in the middle of a blizzard with crazy men shooting at them.

She couldn't really blame any of them.

They didn't understand why she was so hell bent on saving this girl, and that was okay. But she'd made a promise to herself after her twin sister, Ellie, died in a storm just like this, that she would never let another person, let alone another teenaged girl, die on her watch. She'd rather die trying to save them than save herself and leave them behind again.

"I can see the wheels turning in that smart, beautiful head of yours," Gunner said. "Tell me you're not going to do anything stupid."

She couldn't tell him anything, so instead she lowered her head and made him forget everything else once more. Kissing every inch of his face, she planted her lips on his and dove her tongue deep.

Gunner snapped.

He kept her on top of him, but he somehow managed to strip them both of their clothing within minutes. Her pack was by the bed. Thank God she had protection. Harv and JoJo had given it to her as a joke. She'd forgotten it was even in there, until now.

The next thing she knew he was inside her, and she'd never felt more complete.

They moved to a rhythm that was building as fierce as the storm raging outside. He touched and kissed her all over at a frenzied pace, as if he were starving for affection. It warmed her heart and made her think dangerous thoughts.

This wasn't about falling for him.

This was about releasing the built-up sexual tension within her and being afraid that someone was going to kill her and being frustrated over a missing girl. Neither of them seemed to care about anything except satisfying this intense need between them. They couldn't seem to voice their growing feelings for each other, so it was easier to just show how they felt.

They rode a wave of ecstasy together, until they both climaxed and collapsed in a heap of exhaustion. It felt so good to be held, warm and safe in a big, strong man's arms. For now, that was enough. They drifted off to sleep together. At some point during the night, Emma woke up and reached out, but there was nothing there.

Gunner was gone.

He must have gone back to his own room. She felt a moment of emptiness, but shrugged it off. She was a strong, independent woman who didn't need anyone. She tried to fall back to sleep, still recovering from her mild concussion, but gave up at dawn. Exhausted, she acknowledged continuing with this mission wasn't the smartest thing for her to do, but she couldn't stop now.

Emma whipped back the covers and got dressed, checking over her packed backpack. She'd tried to get help, but no one would listen to her. Not even her Dream Team. Left with no choice, she looked around one last time to make sure she didn't forget anything, then she walked out her hotel room door.

She had a plan and supplies and a girl to rescue, if it was the last thing she ever did.

8

THE WINDS HAD DIED DOWN to a walkable pace, the visibility much better than it had been the past couple days. The storm was definitely moving out, which meant the kidnappers would be on the move soon as well. Emma didn't have a death wish, and she wasn't stupid. She planned to keep off the main trails in the woods and follow her map to all the stocked cabins, hoping to get lucky and find the kidnappers and girl hiding out there.

She had her short-wave radio and would call for help as soon as she located them, but if there was a chance to grab the girl herself when they weren't looking, then she would. She also had a weather radio with her, as well as first aid supplies and canned food to last a few days. She chuckled, thinking of her *weapon*.

Her father's old hunting knife. He knew she wouldn't use a gun, so he'd given her the knife when she'd moved away from home. She'd put it in her storm chasing bag but had never had a need for it until now. Her pack was heavy, but she was used to it, and she had her snowshoes. Her grazed arm was getting better, her body not as sore anymore, and the bump on her head was going down. She could do this.

She had to because no one else would.

She set out really early, hoping to get to the first cabin in a couple hours, before anyone noticed her missing. There had to be at least three feet of snow that had fallen during the duration of the storm so far. Even with snowshoes, it was difficult to make her way through the woods. A lot of the tree branches overhead were bare, the sky a cloudy gray with swirling white flakes all around her.

A chill settled over Emma.

The eerie sound of the wind howling made her heart start to race. She squeezed her eyes shut tight, breathing deeply and willing the panic attack away. Memories of she and her sister caught in a deadly storm robbed her of air. The warning times had been too late. All Emma had thought about back then was getting to safety. She hadn't checked to make sure her twin sister was behind her. When she finally did, Ellie had vanished in a nor'easter very much like this one.

Emma blamed herself.

That was why she had dedicated herself to chasing storms, studying them, coming up with better warning systems…all in the name of saving lives, and why this teenage girl out in this storm hit so close to home. Astrid was the same age that Emma and Ellie were when they got lost in the storm.

Her sister's death had been hard on her family, but it was even worse for Emma. They were identical twins, and after Ellie died, Emma felt like a part of her had died as well. Chasing storms was the only way she felt connected to her sister, imagining what Ellie must have felt all alone. Emma took a moment to pull out her compass to make sure she was headed in the right direction.

Northeast.

She clicked the compass closed and shoved it in her

bag. Focusing on putting one foot in front of the other, she trekked deeper into the woods. She spotted a movement up ahead and ducked behind a tree.

Her heart began to pound, and she held her breath for fear the puffs of white steam would give her away. Maybe this had been a bad idea after all. Swallowing hard, she peeked around the edge of the tree and wilted with relief. What on earth was a deer doing out in this storm? They didn't fully hibernate, but during cold weather, they usually hunkered down and moved very little to conserve energy and heat.

Something or someone must have disturbed it.

Taking a deep breath, she kept moving. "This one's for you, Ellie," she said to herself, then blew a kiss up to the sky. If she wasn't mistaken, the first cabin was just up ahead. Several minutes later, she rounded a curve in the path and spotted the wooden structure.

She'd never been more relieved to see anything in her life.

As she approached the building, her heart sank. She was so tired. The door was blocked by at least three feet of wet, heavy snow. It looked empty. She was so cold and desperate. How was she supposed to get inside? She couldn't afford to get down or give up. That's how people died. She slipped off her pack and pulled the small fold-up hand shovel she had attached to the side.

Dropping to her knees, Emma started to dig. Her body was still recovering, but sheer adrenaline gave her strength. Her muscles ached and it felt like forever, but she finally reached the ground and was able to pull the door open just enough to toss her pack inside and then squeeze her body through. Shutting the door behind her, she fell to the floor exhausted and took a moment to catch her breath. Her body felt like a loose rubber band after the adrenaline wore off.

Her brother was right.

She was way too impulsive to the point of putting herself and others in danger. Her obsession to experience what her sister went through so she could feel closer to her wasn't healthy. Harvey and JoJo had told her that many times, but she refused to listen, making excuses that everything she did was for her research and saving lives. She could say she was out here to save Astrid, and that was part of the reason she'd done something so crazy, but not the whole reason.

Being out here alone in a storm gave her way too much time to think. If she were being honest, then she had to admit she felt guilty for surviving. She didn't have a death wish or anything, but maybe she was trying to punish herself. It was too late to go back now. She had to at least try to save Astrid. If she survived this mission, she vowed to stop punishing herself and start living.

Ellie would have wanted that.

Emma started to shiver and realized she needed to get warm. Taking off her snowshoes, she stood and made her way over to the woodstove. Hesitating a moment, she wondered if starting a fire was a smart idea. What if the kidnappers saw the smoke and came after her? She was banking on the snow squalls masking the smoke. She really had no choice if she didn't want to freeze to death.

Thankfully the cabin was still stocked with supplies. Within minutes, she had a fire going. She stripped off her outer gear and shoes, laying the garments out to warm while she stood as close as possible to the heat. Within moments, her body began to warm and so did the room.

Obviously, the kidnappers hadn't found this cabin. After she warmed up and ate something, she planned to head out to try and reach the next cabin before dark.

When she was finally warm, she pulled a can of pork and beans off the shelf and heated it on the stove, keeping her own food supplies safe in her pack for emergencies. Pulling out her map, she sat down to eat and study the path to her next destination.

A scraping sounded outside the door.

Oh, God.

She knew she shouldn't have lit the stove. The kidnappers were the only other people crazy enough to go out in this storm. What if they'd found her? Would they torture her and then kill her? Her gaze darted around the cabin, landing on her pack. Not wasting another second, she scrambled over and pulled her father's hunting knife out then jumped behind the door, heart pounding, just as it opened. Her knife wouldn't be any match against a gun, but it was all she had.

Jabbing twice toward the gut of the intruder, the person reacted with lightning quick moves. One minute she held a weapon in her hand, and the next her arm was twisted behind her back and the weapon was knocked away. In seconds, she lay flat on the floor with the man on top of her. No question about it. This was definitely the dumbest thing she'd ever done, and her survival didn't look so good at the moment.

The weight of her assailant pressed down heavy on her, his heavy breathing close to her ear. "What the hell do you think you're doing?"

She blinked her eyes open. She would know that voice anywhere.

* * *

Gunner was furious with Emma.

After losing himself in making love to her the night before, he couldn't focus. Couldn't think clearly. So, he'd gone to his own room to take a shower and think.

He'd tried to stay away from her, but after she'd almost gotten crushed to death, she'd looked so vulnerable. His willpower had abandoned him, leaving him the vulnerable one.

He didn't like being vulnerable.

First thing this morning, he'd gone to her room to set things straight before she got any romantic notions in her head that this thing between them could be anything more than what it was...

Lust, desire...need.

To his shock, he found her gone, along with her pack and snowshoes. He knew exactly what that meant. She hadn't listened to a word that anyone had said about rescuing the girl being too dangerous to do during the storm, especially on her own.

Another rescue mission was not what he'd come to Coldwater Cove for, especially after the last one had gone so horribly wrong. But protecting others was in his blood. He couldn't let her go after kidnappers alone. Especially not after everything they'd shared. Like it or not, she'd worked her way under his rough hide straight to his heart.

Dammit, if anything happened to her, he wouldn't recover this time.

She might know storms, but she'd never survive without his knowledge. He didn't have time to tell anyone he was going after her or he would risk losing her trail. So, he'd grabbed his own gear and headed out the door. He figured she couldn't be that far ahead of him. He didn't need a map. She was the only crazy fool out there, making it almost too easy for him to track her.

The smoke in the woodstove told him he'd found her. She was literally doing everything wrong. After digging out the snow a little wider to fit his body, he opened the door only to have her thrust a knife at his abdomen.

"I repeat. What the hell do you think you're doing?"

"Gunner?" Emma slapped her hand down on the floor like she used to, when crying uncle after Jack pinned her when wrestling. "Can't breathe," she managed to get out.

Gunner didn't say a word but eased himself off of her so she could roll over. His eyes narrowed to slits, and he kicked her knife further away as he raised a brow, giving her a stare he knew intimidated most people.

She frowned, not intimidated at all. In fact, she looked angry at *him*. "What are *you* doing here? I could have killed you."

He grunted. "Not likely."

"But I had a knife."

"Do you honestly think you're going to stop someone who's twice your size from attacking you by stabbing them in the abdomen? That's just going to piss them off."

"Then what exactly do you suggest I do with a knife?"

"Take away your attacker's ability to fight back. Go for the large muscle groups that allow your attacker to move and wield a weapon."

"Easier said than done."

"Not true."

"Then how do I do it?"

"Cut your attacker long, deep, and accurately," he replied.

Gunner held her stare for a moment longer than he should have judging by the subtle separation of plump lips capable of kissing all common sense out of him. Emma was a challenge he would happily accept if it meant she would be safe. Breaking her spell, he made the decision to demonstrate each move, using the side of his hand as if it were a knife against his body.

"Cut the lower arm, and your attacker can't grab you. Cut the upper arm, and your attacker can't swing an impact weapon. Cut the thigh just above the knee, and your attacker can't move." He reached down and helped her to her feet, this time grabbing her wrist as if she held the knife and pushing her hand hard against his stomach as her bravado slipped. He looked her in the eyes and held her gaze as he finished with, "Puncture the abdomen, you'll just piss your attacker off and leave him free to take his revenge out on you."

Her face flushed bright pink, and she yanked her hand out of his grasp and crossed her arms in front of her. "Lesson learned. I don't like knives any more than I like guns. I think I'll leave the fighting to you, and I'll focus on the science of storms." She pulled out her emergency weather radio and checked the radar. "The storm is moving out. We need to move if we're going to reach the next cabin before dark."

"We aren't going anywhere until morning." He tried the sternest tone of voice he'd ever used. "And then we're going back to town."

This time she raised a brow at him. "*You* can stay here if you want, but *I'm* going to finish what I started."

* * *

"I HOPE she's up by now, Harv," JoJo said when they arrived at Clearwater Commons.

Lucky Emma. This place was a step above staying in the community center with so many other people, but they'd come to the party late, so she couldn't complain. At least they were here now for Emma, and she felt better about that.

"Emma really gave me a scare yesterday. She swears

the shelves falling on her was just an accident, but something seems off to me." JoJo looked up at Harvey. "Does she seem different to you?"

Harvey pushed his glasses up his nose, his clean-shaven face looking serious. The man smelled of fine wine and great food. He had no idea how handsome he really was, but she wasn't about to clue him in and let it go to his head. Still, it was fun getting a rise out of him, which it seemed easier to do lately. She wondered why that was. He'd been acting funny around her since this season's storm chasing had come to an end.

His full lips flattened into a straight line, bringing her back to their conversation. "Something is definitely up," he confirmed. "The kidnappers shot at her in the woods, but it can't be them because they're not in town. Those shelves looked secure to me. How could they possibly fall on their own? But if it wasn't the kidnappers, then it had to be someone in the community center. Who would want to hurt Emma?"

"And why would they want to?" JoJo ran a hand through her messy hair and then scowled at herself. She'd never cared how she looked before in front of Harv. Dropping her hand, she wasn't about to start now. Focusing back on Emma's predicament, she said, "I just don't get it. Everyone in town loves her."

He shrugged. "No sense speculating on something we have no clue about." He started walking. "Let's go see how she's feeling today."

"Sounds good to me." JoJo picked up her pace until she passed him, shooting him a wink over her shoulder.

She was the driver. She refused to come in second place to anyone. He rolled his eyes, and she laughed. *And we're back.* Moments later, they reached Emma's hotel room and knocked on the door.

Silence.

Harvey knocked on the door this time. "Emma? It's Harvey and Jo. You up?"

Nothing.

They both knocked this time, but still nothing.

JoJo tried the doorknob, and was shocked when it opened. "It looks like someone jimmied the lock to get in."

Harvey's eyes widened, and he pushed his way past her. This time she let him.

JoJo searched the room and so did Harvey. She looked at him as panic started to well up inside her. "She's gone."

"Maybe she went to the community center," Harvey said.

"We just came from there. She wasn't there, and neither was Greek god Gunner."

Harvey frowned.

JoJo checked the closet. "Oh, no."

Harvey's frown disappeared, replaced with a worried expression. "What?"

"Her pack is gone, too."

He looked her in the eye. "You don't think after everything that's happened that she would go look for the girl on her own, do you?"

"That's exactly what I think." JoJo sighed long and deep.

The lines on his face formed into ones of determination like when they were about to chase a storm. "You know what we have to do, right?"

"I'll get The Beast. You call the sheriff."

9

Dammit!

I paced the community center, pretending to check out the supplies. Really, I just couldn't sit still. Ever since Michelin Man and his Pink Flamingo had stormed in a few minutes ago and announced Emma Ross was missing, the place had erupted into chaos.

The meddling bitch was playing with fire. I would cut off more than a chunk of her hair if I got my hands on her. She wasn't taking my threats seriously, and it was pissing me off. Did she think this was all a joke?

"Calm down, everyone." Sheriff West raised his voice along with his hands. "Emma was well aware of the risks. She knew what she was getting into by going after the girl while the storm is still going on."

"The storm is weakening," Michelin Man said.

"Yeah, it doesn't take a genius to know as soon as the weather clears, those kidnappers will be gone." Pink Flamingo crossed her arms and stood by his side.

"Alleged kidnappers," Trent corrected. "There's been no request for a ransom or any contact at all. We still don't know for sure if Astrid left willingly." He put his hands on his hips and shook his head.

More chaos sounded throughout the room.

"The girls are getting upset over their friend," Stacy said to her husband, who threw up his hands. She patted his arm. "I'll go speak to them."

"Look, my crews are back out plowing the roads since the storm let up a little," Jack said. "I can take a sled out and look around. Emma knows where the cabins are located. She knows how to survive in a storm. I'm sure that's where she's headed."

"Then she doesn't need you to follow her," Trent countered. "If that storm picks back up, you'll be in whiteout conditions. You won't be able to see where you're going, and you'll down a sled. That's a danger I won't take."

"Look, Sheriff, I understand your concern, but that's my sister we're talking about." Jack rubbed the back of his neck. "I've got an idea. I'll bring Gunner Nash."

"You can't," Pink Flamingo chimed in.

"Why not?" Jack's expression looked puzzled.

"He's missing too," Michelin Man added.

Son of a bitch!

What the hell else could go wrong? It was one thing to have Little Miss Meddler look for the girl on her own. I could have my men easily take her out. But to have a Navy Seal with her was a whole different story. If only the shelves had killed her in the storage room, my men could proceed with the plan as soon as the storm cleared.

I'd warned Emma Ross what would happen if she told anyone about my note. It didn't look like she did. That was the only good thing about today. But she was still out there with the giant. I had to think on this. Find a way to stop them. I couldn't afford for anything else to go wrong. Too much was riding on this.

"You can't go out there alone," Jack's mother spoke up.

"Yeah, son, we can't lose any more children," his father added.

"You won't have to," Pink Flamingo said.

That had my ears perking up.

"We're a team," Michelin Man agreed. "We don't leave our teammates behind.

What the hell did that mean?

"You know how to drive a sled?" Jack asked.

"Honey, I can drive anything with a motor." Pink Flamingo winked at Jack.

"We don't need a sled. The Beast is built to drive over any terrain. JoJo will ride with me," Michelin Man said with a deep voice.

"You're not touching my baby," Pink Flamingo said. "*You* can ride with *me*."

"Then it's settled." Jack rubbed his hands together. "Grab your gear and meet me out front."

Well, hell.

I left the community center to make a phone call. Emma Ross, her giant, her Dream Team, and her brother had forced my hand. They'd be sorry when I got through with them.

It was time for Plan B.

* * *

EMMA AND GUNNER had been walking for quite some time.

"We're getting close to the next cabin," she said, trying not to think about how cold she was. The temperature had dropped since the afternoon. A deep chill had set in and not just because of the weather.

The man's chilly attitude was really getting to her.

Gunner looked up at the sky. "The sun is setting. We need to move quickly if we're going to reach the shelter in time."

They quickened their pace and came upon the same lake where Emma had been shot. The lake that held so many memories for her. She closed her eyes for a minute and just breathed. Emma had to admit, she was relieved to have Gunner with her.

Contemplating their options on the best path to take, she said, "The cabin is just beyond this lake. If we take the time to keep to the woods and walk around the lake, we'll never reach the cabin before dark."

Gunner's eyes never stopped scanning the surrounding woods, his expression grave. "I don't like this."

"I can't say I'm too thrilled about crossing this lake, either, but we don't have a choice." She stepped onto the lake, and her palms started to sweat despite the cold. "I measured the ice last time. We should be fine." The strong winds had blown a lot of the snow off the lake into deeper drifts on land. She walked past the blood stains that were still on the ice, and her mouth went dry.

"I'm right behind you." Gunner's voice was calm and steady.

Emma inhaled a deep breath, and kept moving. With every step she took, she tested the ice. The nor'easter had only made it thicker from the dropping temperatures. They were more than halfway across the lake now.

She picked up the pace until they were drawing near the shore. They were maybe twenty feet out when a loud boom went off close to shore, shaking the ice. Suddenly popping and cracking sounded like popcorn and zippers.

"Don't move!" Gunner shouted.

They were too far away from the other shore to go back, and one step toward the nearest shore would cause them to fall through...

Too late.

The ice gave way beneath Emma's feet and she plunged into the lake, sucking in a breath seconds before she disappeared beneath the ice. The water was so cold it was a shock to her system, making her want to gasp and hyperventilate. She knew enough not to give in to that urge. It would pass in a few minutes. She was disoriented for a moment.

Oh God, the current was pulling at her.

Panic seized her, but a fierce will to live overrode that. The water was so dark, she couldn't see anything. She searched the ice above her but didn't see the hole she fell through. Her heartbeat pounded in her ears. She would run out of air soon. She couldn't die like this. It would kill her parents, Harvey and JoJo would miss her, Jack would never forgive her, Ellie would be disappointed...

Would Gunner even care?

His face swam through her mind's eye. She didn't know exactly what had happened to him on his last mission, but she knew when someone was running away from the pain. She'd been doing it for years.

Suddenly, she felt the presence of her sister.

Looking around, she didn't see anything except eerie darkness, but a strange sense of peace settled over her. She could almost feel her sister hugging her. Looking up one more time, Emma blinked.

There was the hole she'd fallen through.

Kicking hard, Emma swam toward it, her body growing weaker by the second. She couldn't give up. Finally, her head cleared the surface, and she gasped for air. She stuck her arms out on the ice to try to hold on.

"Emma, thank God," Gunner said from ten feet away. He took one step but the ice cracked, so he froze. "Okay, try to stay calm and conserve your heat and energy. You have a while before you will lose consciousness. Listen to me carefully. Don't try to pull yourself straight up. Try to get as horizontal as possible. While kicking your feet, use your elbows to try to get up onto the ice, then pull and kick your way out."

"O-Okay," she said, her teeth chattering so violently she could hardly get the words out.

Her first few attempts failed, but she couldn't stop now. She had to keep trying. Finally, she started to get enough traction going to move some. Little by little, she inched her way out of the water and back onto the ice. Her body was growing numb, and extreme exhaustion was setting in.

"Don't try to stand up. The ice might crack more. Try rolling your way toward me." He'd backed up away from any cracks.

Emma tried but it was taking everything in her to keep her muscles moving. "I-I can't roll anymore. I don't have the strength."

"Yes, you can. Dig deep. Find the strength."

She rolled over a couple more times and then laid her head on the ice, breathing heavy. "I just need to rest for a moment." She closed her eyes.

"Move now!" he barked, and she jumped, complying out of sheer intimidation. "Atta girl." His voice was filled with relief and pride if she wasn't mistaken.

"Happy?" she said weakly when she finally reached him.

"Not even close." He scooped her into his arms and carefully made his way around the cracked ice until they reached the shore.

Gunner moved faster than she thought possible while carrying her and pulling their packs. He didn't speak or stop moving until they reached the cabin. She was shivering so hard now, and confusion started to set in. She was aware that he set her down, dug out the doorway, then the next thing she knew they were inside.

"I'm s-so cold."

"I know. I'm going to fix that; we just can't warm you up too quickly." He gathered wood and then put it in the wood stove and started a fire. He stoked it, and soon the room warmed quickly.

"Wait, what are you doing?" she asked.

He'd already peeled off her drenched coat and hung it on a hook. Then he'd pulled off her hat and mittens and set those by the stove. Now he was unbuttoning her shirt. Just because they'd slept together once, she didn't want him to think he could have her whenever he wanted her. Although, she didn't have the strength to do anything about it at the moment anyway, and honestly, not much desire to stop him, either.

"Taking off your wet clothing to warm you up." His gaze locked on hers. "That's all. I promise."

"Oh," was about all she could manage to say. Her body was trembling so badly, he had to try three times to remove her sweater and bra. He quickly stripped off her boots, jeans and underwear, then wrapped her in a warm, dry blanket and laid her on the couch.

"This will do. You're close enough to the stove without being too hot or heating up too quickly."

"I'm still so cold."

He hesitated only a second, then stripped off his own clothing. Her eyes widened. He didn't look real. His body was a perfectly sculpted masterpiece. His abs had abs. How was that possible? Opening her blanket, he stepped inside and wrapped his naked body around hers, covering them both with the covers.

"Better?"

Emma sighed and snuggled tighter against him as an answer.

He chuckled softly, then she felt him tense a little.

"You scared the hell out of me when you fell beneath the ice." His deep voice rumbled against her cheek resting on his chest. "I thought I'd lost you. That is not a conversation I would want to have with your parents or brother."

"I thought I'd lost me, too, but then I felt her."

"Who?"

"My sister. I don't know how to explain it, I just knew she was with me. That's when I saw the hole I fell through. I know it was her guiding me. She saved me, even though I couldn't save her." A sob caught in Emma's throat.

"Hey, don't be so hard on yourself." He lifted her chin until she looked at him. "It must have been her time to go, but it's obviously not yours."

She touched the cleft in his chin. "I could say the same to you," she said softly as she rested her cheek on his chest once more.

He stiffened. "I don't know what you're talking about."

"Yes, you do. You just don't want to talk about it. That's fine. I don't like talking about my sister's death, either. I'm just saying that whatever happened probably wasn't your fault, either."

"It wasn't." His tone grew cold. "It was someone I trusted with my life who lied to me. That lie put us all in danger and cost a woman and child their lives. I'll never put that much trust in anyone again."

Emma thought about the leader's note in her backpack and the warning to back off or else. She thought of the fact that the lights were on when she'd entered the storage room, but someone shut them off. She'd heard them moving around, but she told everyone the shelves falling on her were an accident. She hadn't outright lied to Gunner.

But a lie by omission was still a lie.

He pulled back the covers and stood up, then searched the bedroom for extra clothes. Returning moments later, he was dressed in long johns and handed her a much smaller pair. He turned his back and searched for food while she quickly got dressed.

"There's some soup I can warm up for us and that's about it. The kidnappers were definitely here. I saw blood stains on the bedroom floor from the bullet I shot him with, so he's wounded. That will slow them down."

"I'm sure they've moved on to the next cabin. We have to find them before they get too far away."

"They're not going anywhere in the dark, and neither are we. And they can't be that far away."

"How do you know?"

"That ice didn't just crack. That boom we heard was an explosive, and there were fresh tracks when we finally reached the shore."

"What if they circle back to try to kill us tonight?"

"They won't. It's too risky in the dark." He grabbed his gun from his pack. "Either way, I don't plan to sleep tonight. Somehow, they knew we were coming. I don't know what they want with the girl, but I do know it can't be good." His gaze met Emma's. "And they're not working alone."

10

Emma felt herself sinking deeper and deeper into the ice-cold water. Everything was growing darker and darker. The deeper she drifted, the smaller the circle of light became. She kicked as hard as she could, but it didn't help. Her strength was fading quickly. Her lungs ached for air, her lips trembling with the desire to open just a little. Seaweed swayed with the current of the water, and a fish swam by.

"It's not your time, Emma," Ellie whispered.

"I can't help it. I'm so tired. I tried," Emma replied.

"Try harder."

"I don't want to die." Emma felt her tears run down her cheeks. There was so much she had to live for. So many dreams she had yet to achieve. What if she died and never had the chance to tell Gunner how she felt? A sob slipped past her lips.

"You're not going to die," Ellie said, her voice growing firmer. "Emma, listen to me. You're okay. I've got you. Emma, do you hear me? Wake up."

Emma blinked her eyes open. "Gunner?"

He had crawled into bed with her and was holding her in his arms. "You were having a nightmare."

"S-So I'm not dead?" Her voice quivered.

"No. Believe me. You're very much alive." His Adam's apple bobbed once.

Very much alive, and naked, and in his arms she realized suddenly. She didn't have any other clothes, so she'd stripped to her birthday suit and dove beneath the heavy covers. He'd made it clear that he planned to stay up and keep watch out in the living room all night. And he had...

Until now.

"I'm sorry," she said.

"It's okay." He started to sit up.

"Don't leave me," she quickly grabbed onto him. "I don't want to be alone. I don't want to sleep or dream or think." She stared into his eyes, and another tear leaked out of hers. "It's too scary."

"You're safe. I've got you," he said. "And I'm not going anywhere."

"Distract me," she said, her lips parting as she stared at his.

He groaned. "I don't think that's a good idea. You're injured."

"Then don't think. I feel better." She bit her bottom lip. If she couldn't tell him how she felt, maybe she could show him. "Please. I need you. I-I need to feel alive."

The war waging in his eyes finally gave way, and he slowly lowered his head to press his lips against hers with his eyes still open. She was helpless to look away. Slipping his tongue inside, he deepened the kiss, exploring every inch of her mouth. She moaned; her eyelids fluttering closed as her stomach did a funny little flip.

Last time had been wild and full of need. A burning desire for each other that couldn't be contained. This time, this large powerful intense man was being so gentle and tender. She felt worshipped and cherished.

It had been a long time since she'd felt safe in a man's arms.

It was easier to take care of herself than to lean on someone else. Depend on someone else. Need someone else. She couldn't risk growing attached because what if he walked away, and she lost him, too?

As if he could feel her thinking, he slid his lips down her neck, and her mind went blank. All she could do was feel. His hand cupped her breast, teasing her nipple until she whimpered for more. Running his tongue down the curve of her breast, he circled her nipple and drew her deep into his mouth, sucking hard until she cried out in ecstasy. She gripped his naked shoulders as he slid down her stomach.

When had he taken off his shirt?

She couldn't think. All she could do was squirm with need and desire. She clawed at his shoulders, whispering his name over and over. He ran his palm down the length of her stomach and cupped her womanhood. Slowly slipping a finger inside her, and then two, he stroked her insides in circular motions, getting her ready for him. She'd seen him naked. He was indeed a very large man.

The pressure began building once more, and she started writhing on the sheets, muttering his name in between whimpers. He slid his body down the length of her in the same path his hand had taken, and then he paused, looking up into her eyes as he parted her and dove his tongue deep.

Emma screamed.

Spasms ripped through her body, heat exploding throughout her insides, sending tingles through her muscles. Her head whipped back and forth on the pillow; her eyes squeezed tight. She'd never wanted another human being so badly. Not just his body. His soul. She'd been alone for far too long. She needed to feel connected, to give her something to hold onto.

She needed to feel loved.

Grabbing his head, she tugged at him until he slid back up the length of her. She whispered, "More. I need more."

He didn't say anything, but he didn't have to. His eyes said he felt the same way. He rolled away and slipped off his pants then grabbed some condoms from inside his pack. It didn't surprise her that he had protection with him. The man had everything a human being might possibly need inside that pack.

He joined her back on the bed and handed the condom to her, his beautiful hazel eyes growing hooded with desire.

Feeling bold, she rolled him onto his back and ran her fingertips down his muscular body. His skin was silky smooth as it stretched tight over a ripped abdomen. Even in a relaxed state, the man was a work of art. With every muscle she touched, he twitched. She trailed her fingers lower and circled the length of him with her fingertips.

"Emma," he said in a deep husky voice.

She could feel the same desire, same passion, same need for her that she had for him. All she wanted to do was give him the same pleasure he gave to her. She wrapped her hand around him tightly and ran it up and down the long length of him until she felt him quiver. His need for her was rolling off him in waves. Locking her eyes on his, she lowered her head and took the length of him deep into her mouth, sucking hard.

He gripped the bedsheets with his fists, his face unmasked, revealing his struggle for control as he hissed out a warning, "Emma, now."

Having mercy on him and wanting him as badly as

he wanted her, she sat up and rolled the condom down his penis. She could feel him shaking on the verge of losing control. The second she finished, he picked her up as if she weighed nothing and set her down on top of him in one swift motion until he was deep inside of her.

She gasped, feeling the thrill shoot straight through her core. Hearing him suck in a breath was more arousing than anything he could have said. They both stilled, reveling in the wonder of being joined together as one, their eyes locked on each other as they caught their breath.

After a long moment, Emma began to move.

Slowly at first until his hands settled on her hips and he urged her on faster. She felt the tension build inside of her once more. Feeling free and so alive, she let go of all her inhibitions, whipping her head back and forth and letting all her feelings transform her face.

"You're magnificent," he whispered, and that was her undoing.

She rode the wave until her every muscle in her body tensed and quivered. With one final cry of pure joy, she collapsed on top of him. He ran his hands up and down her back over and over until her breathing finally returned to normal. He wasn't the first man she'd had sex with, but something felt different with him. More intense. More connected.

Special....

"My turn," she heard in her ear.

Lifting her head to look at him, she sucked in a breath. His eyes blazed with desire. "Oh, I thought we were done." Was that her voice?

"Darlin', we're just getting started."

* * *

GUNNER STARED into the eyes of the green-eyed goddess lying naked on his chest with messy hair and swollen lips. He gave a low growl and flipped her onto her back. Rolling on another condom, he lifted her legs over his shoulders and slid his engorged, throbbing penis inside of her. Fuck, he nearly came undone right then and there. She was so tight and warm, clenching him over and over.

"Don't move, baby. Just…wait a minute." He squeezed his eyes tight for a moment, on the verge of losing it.

She didn't move an inch for several beats, and then he felt her cradle his face with her palms. His eyes slowly opened and he stared into her emerald pools. He didn't like feeling vulnerable with people. Getting close to someone meant risking them betraying you, and he couldn't go through that again.

He could admit he'd been drawn to Emma right from the first moment he'd met her. She made him mad and confused and frustrated and happy all at the same time. The point was, she made him *feel*, and that hadn't happened in a long time. Her nearly dying had scared the hell out of him, and her nightmare had tortured him.

He'd only wanted to comfort her.

To find her naked in bed had nearly undone him, but he'd held back until she'd begged him not to leave her. Begged him to love her with her eyes. No matter how hard he tried to keep his distance, her eyes looked straight into his soul and tugged at his heart.

He could no more resist her then than he could now.

Leaning down, he kissed her deeply, swirling his tongue in time with the motion of his slow sensual thrusts. She bit his lip and clawed at his head until he moved faster. Reaching down between them, he found her nub of desire and stroked his thumb over it. She sucked in a breath, and he did it again until she screamed his name.

Letting go, he matched her pace until he could no longer think. The pressure built throughout his body, his muscles flexing and releasing, until finally his release crashed over him. He crushed her to him and shouted her name, then fell on top of her, rolling away and taking her with him until she rested on his chest.

Their hearts beat in unison.

She was an incredible woman. He didn't think she realized just how much she had to offer someone. She was stubborn and headstrong, but so fierce and loyal. She would do anything to help others to the point of being impulsive and putting herself in danger. All because she was passionate about storms and justice and life and...love.

Doubts crept in as she fell asleep in his arms. She stirred up so many emotions in him, but he didn't want to hurt her. What if she wanted more than this one night? He didn't know if he was capable of trusting someone fully again. He still had PTSD he had to work through. It wouldn't be fair of him to saddle her with his baggage.

Closing his eyes, he tried not to think about it. He couldn't dwell on something that might not even happen. She might be fine with one night. She had her own issues to work through as well. If they only had tonight, then he planned to make the most of it. He lay there for hours, letting her sleep, until the first rays of dawn started lighting the sky.

Scooping her into his arms, he carried her to the bathroom. She murmured a little, then snuggled deeper into his arms. He turned on the shower until the room filled with steam and then he stepped inside with her.

Sliding her down the length of him, he kissed her lips until she woke up.

"Good morning," he whispered against her lips, trailing his fingertips over her nipple and down her stomach until he cupped her sex. Parting the folds, he slipped two fingers inside and rotated them in a circle, swirling his thumb over the top of her.

She squirmed against his hand and began to pant. "Great morning," she managed. "More please."

"I don't have a condom, but I can promise you, I'm clean."

"Me too. I don't care about the condom." Her eyes locked with his. "I need to feel you inside of me. All of you."

Lifting her high and hard against him, he pressed her back against the shower wall and plunged deep. "God, you feel so good." He pressed his forehead to hers and just held her there, joined to him, she was his.

"You feel amazing." She kissed his neck and face.

He began to move. He would pull out in time, but right now, he needed to feel her, too. Damn, she felt like hot syrup, her insides melting around him so sweetly. She locked her legs around him and held him tight, running her hands over every inch of his skin that she could reach.

Kissing and licking his neck, shoulders, and chest, he clenched his jaw to hold in his release, thrusting deeper and deeper until she reached her peak. Watching her orgasm over and over was pleasure enough for him.

She fell limp on him. He held her in his arms, his hands beneath her bare bottom, still locked together as one. He was throbbing so hard it hurt.

"Put me down," she said softly.

He regretfully withdrew from her and immediately felt the loss. She slid slowly down the front of him until her unsteady feet touched the floor. Kissing her way down the length of him, lower and lower until she reached her knees, she finally looked up into his eyes as she slid her mouth over his engorged, throbbing manhood.

"Christ." He panted. "Baby, you're killing me. I'm not going to be able to hold back much longer."

"I don't want you to," she said, then licked the top of him before taking him inside her mouth once more.

His legs shook and he tried to pull out, but she grabbed his bare ass and pushed him against the shower wall while she lathered him with love. He filled his hands with her hair as her head moved back and forth, faster and faster, until he couldn't take it anymore. His muscles stiffened and his butt cheeks clenched as he shouted out her name on his release.

She slid back up the length of him and hugged him, resting her cheek against his chest. He hadn't expected her to do that for him. She was so selfless and giving, always making sure other people were happy, he couldn't help but start to fall for her.

And that was dangerous territory.

He could feel his walls start to go up as he shut off the shower and reached out to grab their towels. He didn't want to be this way, but he couldn't help himself. Handing her one, she looked at him with eyes filled with something he was afraid to identify. Fear gripped his throat, making it hard to speak.

"Sun's up. We should probably get dressed and head out." He smiled but knew it didn't quite reach his eyes.

She nodded once and turned away to dry off, but not before he saw the confusion and sadness fill her eyes. Cursing silently, he gave her some space and left the bathroom to get dressed. Moments later, she emerged dressed as well.

"I'm going to grab any extra supplies I can find," he

said in a voice that was purposely all business. "Meet you out front in five."

"Okay," she replied, but the light in her eyes had dimmed, replaced by one of wariness and regret.

Damned if he wasn't the one who'd put it there.

11

THE NEXT DAY the blizzard had finally stopped. Jack raced across the snow on his sled with Harvey and JoJo following him in The Beast. That machine was like a military tank and pretty much could cover any terrain. It could traverse land and sea. The only thing it couldn't do was fly. From what he was discovering about JoJo, he wouldn't be surprised if she found a way to make it do that as well.

She was one hell of a mechanic.

His lips turned up when he thought of the little spitfire. She was entertaining, that was for sure. He couldn't quite tell if there was anything going on romantically between Harvey and her. That was one big boy, but he didn't seem the fighting type. Not that Jack wanted to fight the man, but he had a feeling if push came to shove, Harvey wouldn't hesitate to stake his claim on JoJo.

If Jack were being honest, he knew he didn't want a relationship with anyone. He didn't want to get married and didn't want children. He knew first-hand how heartbreaking it was to lose someone you loved. His parents had never fully recovered after losing Ellie. None of them had. He set his jaw.

He couldn't let them lose Emma, too.

Jack, Harvey, and JoJo had made it to the first cabin just after dark the night before, and Jack had been relieved to see signs that Emma and Gunner had been there. He could only guess they'd made their way to the second cabin next. The last of the storm had covered their tracks, but Jack's gut told him that was where his sister would go.

Rounding a bend in the trail, he finally reached the cabin. He shut the sled off and dismounted. JoJo pulled up next to him and cut the engine of The Beast. They got out and joined Jack in entering the cabin.

"They were definitely here," Jack said. "The door to the cabin was dug out, and the wood stove is still warm."

JoJo came from the bedroom, her lips twisting into a lopsided smirk. "They left the bed unmade. There's only one in there, by the way."

"Okay, okay. I don't need to hear that." Jack waved off her words with his hand and kept looking around the cabin.

"There's no food left." Harvey closed the cupboard door. "That's a lot for only two people to eat in one night." He cleaned his glasses with a napkin and put them back on, then pulled his fur-lined hood back up.

"The kidnappers were here before them." Jack held up an orange hairband. "Emma's never been a fan of the color orange. This has to be Astrid's."

"That's a good sign. Maybe the girl is still alive." JoJo tightened her hot pink coat over her matching snow pants and adjusted her earmuffs.

Jack eyed the Dream Team and silently chuckled. The two were quite a pair.

"Hopefully, she is still alive." He lost his grin. "But for how long?" Jack looked JoJo in the eyes. Lavender. What an unusual color.

She winked, as if reading his mind. As if she knew the effect she had on men and enjoyed messing with them. "All the more reason to hurry. Right, Harv?"

Harvey nodded. "They're all on foot. We can't be that far behind them. Maybe we can catch up with Emma and Gunner at least. Together we all stand a better chance of succeeding in getting the girl back."

"Let's roll," Jack said.

They all went back outside and were ready to leave, when JoJo shielded her eyes and looked in a different direction than they had come.

"What's in that direction?" she asked.

Jack looked to where she pointed. "The lake. Why?"

She started walking instead of answering him, so he and Harvey followed.

She came to a stop and picked up an item. "This is Emma's red scarf. I would recognize it anywhere. We always wear bright colors in case we get separated when chasing storms." JoJo looked Harvey up and down and shook her head. "Except for Harv, here. He wears white. I told him white is *not* a color, but he said it's bright and can be seen in a storm." She snorted. "A tornado, maybe. A lot of good it does him in a blizzard."

Jack laughed.

Harvey ignored them both.

Walking past them with long strides, Harvey headed to the lake. They hurried after him but didn't say another word. Jack had the same instinct that Harvey must have. Something had gone down at the lake.

He could feel it.

When they reached the lake, they all started looking around. The sun was shining high in the sky, the area stunning with the fresh coat of pristine snow. This felt the same as when Ellie had gone missing. They'd found her the day the storm ended in a place just like this on a day just as beautiful. He swallowed past the lump in his throat.

Mother Nature could be a cruel bitch.

Harvey bent down and studied the ground. He pointed to a piece of metal. "I'm no expert, but this looks like a piece of an explosive."

That got Jack's attention.

He had a sinking feeling that Emma was in trouble. He looked out over the water, and his heart skipped a beat. "And that looks like a big hole in the ice." He pointed, fearing the worst. "The question is, are we too late?"

* * *

"Make sure you keep on the main trail," Gunner said to Emma. "That red coat of yours stands out from a mile away."

He was trying like hell to act like they had before she'd turned his world upside down into something he sure as hell wasn't ready for, but that was turning out to be impossible to ignore. He couldn't stop remembering the touch of her skin, as soft as rose petals. The smell of her fragrance, as stirring as any aphrodisiac. The hot, tight feeling of being deep inside of her like nothing he'd ever felt before.

But mostly the scary-as-hell feeling of being connected at the soul. With anyone else, he would have been spooked enough to walk. Not with Emma. With her, he craved that connection, needing it as much as he needed air to breathe.

"In my line of work, standing out is the point. Storm chasing is a dangerous profession." Her words snapped him out of his dangerous thoughts. "I need to be seen if I get separated from my group, and my red coat works beautifully for that." Her tone sounded cold and terse, definitely not warm and passionate like it had only a couple hours ago, which actually made it easier for him to focus on their mission and not the romantic thoughts he had no business thinking. A woman like Emma, no matter how she made him feel, deserved a hell of a lot more than a broken Navy Seal.

Dangerous thoughts only led to trouble.

"Well, in *my* line of work, I need to blend in," he replied in his usual calm, logical, non-emotional tone. "You should have thought about the mission you were headed on and packed a little more appropriately."

"I didn't think about that," she admitted.

"That much is obvious. You tend to be impulsive. Haven't you ever heard good things come to those who wait?"

She blew out a frustrated breath. "Well, someone has to do something when the situation calls for it, or things don't get done."

"Logically, the sheriff would have gone after the girl one day later when the storm ended, with a lot more reinforcements, I might add." He shot her the same look he would shoot an unreasonable child. "If only you had waited."

She threw her hands in the air. "You men and your ridiculous *logic*. Sometimes you need to throw caution to the wind and act. If we had waited one day later, we would have missed out on any chance of finding the girl."

"There's no point in talking about the right or wrong way in rescuing the girl now. The damage is already done, and we're already here."

Emma rolled her eyes at him and looked around as they walked. "We're getting closer now. I can feel it."

"The one who is injured is slowing them down." Gunner inspected a broken tree branch that had blood on it. "These guys are no amateurs. You'd better hope they don't decide the girl isn't worth it, cut their losses, and move on."

"Oh, believe me, they won't do anything unless they're told to," she said with such certainty and a strange look on her face.

His gaze shot to hers and locked on. "Told to? By who? What exactly are you trying to say, Ms. Ross?"

"Nothing, Mr. Nash." Her cheeks flushed pink. "I mean, it's like you said before. Maybe they have someone they answer to, is all I meant."

"Maybe." He eyed her suspiciously. Why was she blushing? "They definitely knew we were coming for them or they wouldn't have set up that explosive. All the more reason we should have waited for backup."

"I thought we were done with that conversation." She picked up the pace. "I don't know how they could have known where we would be."

"It's logical we would head for the safety cabins just like they did, but we're behind them. There is no way they could know we're out searching for them. Someone had to have tipped them off."

"I have no clue about that, but the storm is over. They had to expect people would start looking for Astrid."

"That's true if the storm had been over when you started out and I followed you, but it wasn't." He studied her body language and didn't like what he saw. "It's not logical to expect anyone would be crazy enough to do that."

"There you go again." She picked up a stick and kept walking. "You and your logic. Life isn't logical. Astrid's father is a powerful man with money, and his daughter is out in a blizzard with two men who have a gun."

"But he doesn't know this area or storms or survival. It's not logical that he would go on a rescue mission."

She stopped and pointed her stick at him. "But it *is* logical that he might pay someone to go on that mission for him."

"I'm still not buying it." He shook his head and scanned the area, always on alert. Hell, he was that way even when he wasn't on a mission. It was second nature to be watchful after having done it for so long. "I think they have someone on the inside who got word to the kidnappers that we were tracking them."

"Daylight's wasting. We'd better pick up the pace." Emma walked ahead of him, limping a little, but trying her best to walk faster.

He couldn't help but wonder if something more was bothering her than his abrupt change of emotion with the light of day. Something was definitely up with her, and he didn't plan to stop being *logical* until he figured it out.

***

AFTER WALKING AN HOUR, they stopped for a break. Emma sat on a log in the forest, eating beef jerky and drinking water. She was exhausted and not in a good way. She didn't understand Gunner's abrupt change of attitude. He'd literally gone from hot to cold as soon as the sun had come up.

How could he ignore her after all they had shared?

She missed the way his eyelids grew hooded when they looked at her. The way her body came alive when he touched her flesh so softly. The way his smell set her body on fire. The way he completed her when he filled her so deeply and made them one. She'd never felt so safe and warm and protected as she did when he held her in his big strong arms.

How could he give her all of that and then yank it away so coldly?

She hadn't planned on asking for anything more than last night from him, but he hadn't even given her a chance to say that. He'd made assumptions and then cut her off. That wasn't fair to either of them. She had fear of loss, and he had trust issues. Things would never work between them, especially if he found out she knew the kidnappers were working with a mole back in Coldwater Cove and didn't tell him.

She couldn't risk the leader ordering Astrid killed.

If Emma kept her mouth shut, no one would be looking for a third party. And in her defense, she'd thought she would be going alone and calling for help once she found them. She hadn't counted on Gunner following her.

They were so close to reaching Astrid. That's all Emma cared about. Saving the girl to make up for not saving her sister. That had been the one thought that kept driving her to continue. She finished her jerky and pulled out her map. They were almost there. She stood up and pulled out her compass, walking in a circle and then stopping when she hit the direction she wanted to go.

North.

She grabbed her pack and started walking.

Gunner emerged from the trees and fell into step beside her as if he'd been watching her. "I followed their tracks a little way. There are still three sets of snowshoe tracks, and they stop often, which indicates the man who is wounded isn't doing well. There are a few spots where there looks to be a struggle, as if the girl put up a fight. That leads me to believe Astrid did not run away from the school and go willingly with these men." His gaze settled on Emma's. "She was definitely taken. The question is why."

"And what are we going to do about it?"

* * *

"I THOUGHT you said you took care of them, Nikolai?" I asked through my short-wave radio while I sat in my car. I couldn't take a chance of anyone overhearing me. I'd equipped those idiots with a radio of their own when we'd first made our plan and told them what frequency to tune into so we could stay in touch.

"I did, Boss. I took care of the problem while Boris stayed with the girl at the other cabin. He's useless anyway with his bullet wound."

"Emma Ross is still alive," I ground out.

There was a brief hesitation. "There's no way she can be. I set off the detonation and then saw the ice crack. I saw her fall through the ice and disappear below it with my own eyes."

"You were stupid enough to stick around?" God, I'd hired such incompetent fools. I really should have just handled the matter myself right from the start.

"No, no. I was far enough away and looked through my binoculars before I headed on to the cabin where Boris and the girl are."

"Whatever." I slammed my fist down on my steering wheel. "The point is, you failed. Emma Ross is still very much alive."

"How do you know?"

"Don't question my authority. I have my ways. Just know they're on the move as we speak, drawing closer to you."

"Shit."

"And they're not alone."

"What does that mean?"

"Her brother and her storm chasing team headed out after them. They can't be too far behind."

"Do you want me to abort the mission and retreat?"

"No. I have too much riding on this deal. You can't

outrun them with Boris injured. Do your job and get rid of them."

Another hesitation. "*All* of them?"

"Yes, all of them. We can't afford any witnesses." I paused to let my meaning sink in. "And you can't afford to disappoint me again."

12

"WATCH WHERE YOU'RE GOING, JO." Harvey gripped the *Oh Shit* bar in The Beast as JoJo drove the monster tank on the trail through the woods, giving good 'ole Jack a run for his money on the snow mobile. He was Emma's brother, and a nice enough guy, but Harvey didn't like the way he looked at JoJo.

"Don't be such a wimp, Harv." JoJo snorted. "I don't want to lose to Jack or any man. You have no idea how hard it is for a female driver to be taken seriously. I've been fighting that battle my whole life."

"Lose to him? If you get any closer, you'll be on top of him."

"Now, there's a thought." She grinned.

Harvey frowned.

JoJo loved testing his patience. He couldn't tell if she was into Jack or not. Hell, he had no idea if she was into him, either. Just when he'd figured out he had a thing for her, she had to go and flirt with another man.

A *handsome* man.

It didn't matter. JoJo might not feel the same way about Harvey at all, and a relationship would compromise their team. Harvey chalked up his feelings to the long storm season they'd had this year. When they weren't chasing storms together, they all shared a house. That was a lot of togetherness.

He didn't regret his choice of profession. Storm chasing was thrilling work, but it didn't leave much time to have a normal life. He was a normal human being who had needs. It was only logical that, in spending so much time with each other, romantic feelings could develop. But to start a relationship would be reckless.

Emma was reckless enough for all of them.

"We don't need to go this fast," Harvey said to JoJo. "Emma and Gunner are on foot. We've probably already passed them if they're keeping to the woods for safety's sake. We're sitting ducks out here."

"Sitting ducks surrounded by bullet-proof armor." JoJo laughed and kept driving just as fast.

Harvey sighed, giving up.

Jack suddenly slammed on his breaks and jerked the sled to the side of the road.

Harvey screamed. Actually *screamed* in a pitch so high his throat would be sore for a week. JoJo missed the sled by a mere inch, expertly maneuvering The Beast through a one-eighty turn, and coming to a stop facing Jack on the side of the road.

She looked up at Harvey and winked. "You gonna be okay, there, Big Boy?"

He scowled and opened the hatch, climbing out to suck in a huge unsteady breath. His heart hammered against his chest so hard he could swear he felt a rib crack. A blast of cold air hit him in the face, reminding him of their purpose in being out in the woods.

"What's wrong?" he hollered to Jack.

"I see something through the woods. It's lime green like the colors Astrid wears when skiing." Jack squinted as he pointed through the woods. "We can't fit through that section of the trail on our vehicles. We'll have to walk."

Harvey nodded and turned to tell JoJo, but she was already outside. Grabbing his camera and video equipment that he used to document a storm, he got out to join them. Jack eyed him funny. Harvey held up his camera. "I figured we might want to document what we find for the police."

"Good call." Jack started walking and motioned for them to follow, carefully making his way through the woods.

JoJo sped up and passed him like the pink panther that she was.

She always had to be first on a scene. The woman had two speeds. Run and run faster. As much as she frustrated him, Harvey couldn't stop the corners of his lips from turning up. Hoisting his camera, he turned it on and picked up the pace. Moving was difficult, even with snowshoes on.

"Hey, there it is." JoJo pointed at a green object. "It looks like a hat." She started to walk toward it.

Jack caught up to her and grabbed her arm to get her to stop. "Hey, wait a minute. We don't know what—"

"I'll get it!" Harvey surged past them.

He was normally never impulsive, over thinking things to the point of driving his teammates crazy, but this time he wanted to be the hero in JoJo's eyes. He took a couple big leaps through the deep snow and reached for the hat. The second he stepped onto what looked to be normal snow, he realized the ground wasn't firm. The snow-covered tarp he'd stepped on gave way.

"No!" Jack yelled.

"Harv!" JoJo shouted at the same time.

Everything happened so fast, yet it felt like his life was flashing before him in slow motion. His arms windmilled, and his eyes locked with JoJo's. Her face was the last thing he saw before he plunged into a deep dark hole.

Thud.

Harvey screamed for the second time that day. Burning pain shot through his thigh. What the hell had just happened? He reached down and realized he'd fallen on a tree branch that had been sharpened into a spear. His hand was covered in blood already. His eyes grew huge, and fear settled deep into his bones.

Looking around, Harvey realized he was at the bottom of a manmade hole in the ground. Like a freshly dug grave. He swallowed dryly. There were makeshift spears poking up from the bottom all around him.

One had barely missed his abdomen.

He'd almost died. He was too young to die, especially after not telling JoJo how he felt. What did he have to lose? The real reason he hadn't told her wasn't because it would make work complicated. He'd been a coward, plain and simple. He squeezed his eyes shut for a moment, realizing he was still alive. Realizing he had a second chance.

Realizing it wasn't too late.

"Hey, man, are you okay?" Jack looked over the edge above him.

"No," Harvey hissed through his teeth, the pain becoming unbearable now that the shock of what had happened was wearing off.

"Oh, my God, Harv. I thought you were dead." JoJo's eyes were huge as she stared down at him.

"You and me both," he ground out.

"What happened?" she asked, looking troubled and worried.

"This was no accident. This was a trap," Harvey said. "Don't get any closer in case the edge caves in. I really don't want to be buried alive."

Jack shined a flashlight down into the hole. "Oh, hell."

"Is that a stick poking out of your leg, or is it a bone?" JoJo gaped. "Oh, man, I'm gonna be sick." She started gagging.

"Well, turn away. Don't puke over the hole, Jo." Harvey made a few gagging sounds of his own. "If you vomit on me, that will kill me for sure."

Jack cursed. "Look at how many spears there are? You're one lucky dude. A couple inches more to the left, and you'd be—"

"Yeah, I know. Can we stop talking about that?" He felt the blood drain away from his face.

"Stay with me, man," Jack said as he clapped his hands. "We don't need you passing out."

"We have to get him out of there," JoJo said to Jack. There has to be a way. "Can you stand, Harv?"

"No. I'm stuck on the ground with a spear impaled through my thigh like a pig on a spit. Oh, God, I'm going to die here," he added, trying not to panic.

"Snap out of it, Harv. You're not going to die. You're too stubborn for that. Let's think clearly now." JoJo snapped her fingers. "I know. We'll go for help."

"And leave me alone?" His eyes sprang wide. "I've seen the movies. I'll either bleed to death or get eaten by wolves."

"Okay, I'll stay with you, you stubborn fool." She slapped her forehead. "Jack can go for help. Someone has to."

"Not stubborn. Just realistic. You might be one hell

of a driver, but no offense, you don't stand a chance against a hungry wolfpack."

"JoJo get down and be quiet," Jack said. "I hear something."

"Great," Harvey whispered. "Now we're *all* going to die."

* * *

GUNNER STOPPED SUDDENLY in the woods and listened. The normal sounds of the few wildlife that weren't hibernating could be heard, but otherwise there was an eerie silence. Eerie and telling. They'd kept off the trail and stayed inside the woods, trying to avoid the road so they wouldn't be seen.

"Why are we stopping?"

"We're not alone."

Emma's face paled. "What should we do? Run in a zigzag? Lay in a ditch? Stop, drop and roll?" She shook out her mittened hands. "I'm nervous."

"I couldn't tell," he said quietly, his gaze taking in his surroundings. "Stay behind me and be as quiet as you can."

"Okay." For once she didn't argue, she just did what he told her to by getting behind him and not talking.

Keeping low to the ground, they slowly made their way from tree to tree. Each time, he took a moment to assess the situation before moving on to his next target. Gunner froze. After a long pause, he finally whispered, "Stay here."

"No way."

He gave her his most intimidating look, but she simply crossed her arms stubbornly. So much for doing what she was told. He should have known her compliance wouldn't last long. He grunted in frustration, but kept moving.

"That's JoJo." Emma popped out from behind him and pointed ahead. "I would recognize that bright pink snowsuit anywhere. What in the world are they doing out here?" She held up her hands ready to shout to her friend.

Gunner stood up and covered her mouth. "Have you ever heard of the element of surprise?" He dropped his hands and gaped at her. "If the kidnappers are there, you just gave us away."

"Look." She pointed again, ignoring his comment. "All I see are JoJo and Jack lying on the ground." Her mouth fell open. "Oh, no. Do you think they're dead? And where's Harvey? I'll never forgive myself is something happened to them."

"We won't know anything just standing here." Gunner scanned the area but didn't see anything. He pulled his gun just in case and moved forward.

"Are you guys alone?" Gunner called out when they grew closer.

Jack lifted his head up, looking relieved as he nodded. "Thank God it's you guys. I thought it might be the kidnappers."

"Harv is hurt." JoJo chewed her bottom lip as she sat up and pointed at the hole behind them.

"Harvey, I'm coming," Emma started running forward.

Would she ever learn from her mistakes?

Gunner caught her by the waist and pulled her back against him. "That's a good way to get you both killed."

She stilled immediately.

"This trap was obviously set for you two." Jack pointed down into the hole behind him. "They booby trapped the hole with wooden spears. Harvey's lucky. His thigh is impaled, but that's it."

"What if he bleeds to death?" Emma asked, looking shaky.

"That's not likely as long as we leave the stick in his leg," Gunner said.

"What? You want to leave me impaled?" Harvey called up weakly from below. "I want this thing out of my leg now."

"I understand how you must feel, but we don't know if it struck an artery. If we remove it, you could bleed out before we have time to get you back to town for help. We need to move quickly before the kidnappers come back."

Gunner slipped his pack off and retrieved a rope, harness, and his survival knife. Looking around the area, he found a thick tree close by and tied off the rope. Once he was sure it was secure, he slipped on his harness and rappelled down the hole carefully to miss the other spears. Once his feet struck bottom, he squeezed Harvey's shoulder.

Harvey's eyes sprang open, looking dazed. Most likely from shock.

"Hang in there. I'll have you out soon."

"Nothing's ever sounded better." He winced and let out a moan. "This burns like a mother."

"I bet it does. I'm going to have to saw through both sides of this stick so we can hoist you up." Gunner looked him in the eyes. "I'll try to be as careful as I can, but I'm not going to lie. It's going to hurt like hell."

"Just because I don't like to fight, doesn't mean I'm not tough, contrary to popular belief." Harvey looked up at JoJo and Emma.

"I never doubted that for a minute," Gunner said. "You're nearly as big as I am." He found a smaller piece of wood and handed it to Harvey. "Bite down on this."

Harvey nodded once and put the wood in his mouth.

Gunner worked as quickly as he could with the jagged side of his survival knife. Harvey's face pinched and body tensed, but he didn't let out a single sound. Once Gunner finished, only a couple inches of the spear stuck out of either side of Harvey's thigh. The man was sweating something fierce despite the frigid temperatures.

"You good?"

Harvey glanced up at JoJo then nodded, squaring his big shoulders.

Gunner helped him to stand, then he put the harness on him. He instructed Jack to pull on the rope from up top while Gunner used a pulley system and pulled on the rope from down below until Harvey reached the top.

The man was solid as a rock. It took Jack, JoJo, and Emma to pull Harvey the last few feet over the edge.

"Show-off," JoJo said, but her voice was soft.

"Just taking one for the team," Harvey managed to get out through his clenched teeth, but his color didn't look good.

Jack frowned. "We need to get him to a hospital." He looked at Gunner. "Keys are in the sled." Emma had told him what happened on the ice, and he was naturally worried sick about her now. "I think it's time we all got the hell out of here, given everything that's happened, don't you?" He looked at Emma.

She didn't say anything, so he looked back at Gunner.

"Take that and bring Emma home. Harvey and I will ride with JoJo."

Gunner nodded once and helped Jack get Harvey situated in The Beast. Once he was stabilized, they left.

Gunner turned to Emma. "You ready?"

"I'm not going back without Astrid." She crossed her arms and stood defiantly.

"I figured as much, but I didn't plan on going back. I still don't think coming out here alone was a good idea, but what's done is done. Besides, it's personal now. Once I commit to a mission, I don't quit until I see it through."

And he sure as hell didn't plan to leave another innocent victim behind.

13

Emma held on tight to Gunner, feeling his muscles bunch and tighten as they flexed and released. They circled around toward the next cabin, staying out of sight. It was clear the kidnappers knew they were being followed. One of them kept doubling back and setting traps in an attempt to kill them.

Emma could only pray that Astrid was still alive.

She was banking on the leader's plan being too important to him to kill. She reasoned, if it wasn't, then Astrid would already be dead and the kidnappers wouldn't keep trying to kill her and Gunner. But they were getting closer to the border and the ocean. They could still get away for good if Emma and Gunner didn't overtake them first.

Gunner didn't know there was a leader for sure, he only suspected. If he knew Emma had kept the knowledge that she'd been warned to back off and not tell anyone or the girl would die, he would be furious with her. Emma hadn't wanted anyone to come along for fear of putting them in danger.

It wasn't one of her smarter decisions.

She couldn't help if Gunner had followed her. He'd done that all on his own, but she was indebted to him and felt guilty that she hadn't told him about the note yet. It was a scary thought knowing she might have died if it wasn't for his help after falling through the ice, but at least no one else would have gotten hurt.

Her heart ached to know poor Harvey had nearly died in a trap meant for her. She knew she could survive in a storm and had only wanted to find the kidnapper's location before it was too late. Then she'd had every intention of radioing for help in retrieving Astrid.

How had everything gone so wrong?

She hadn't expected the kidnappers to turn the tables and start hunting them. Why hadn't they made any demands or asked for ransom money? None of this situation made any sense. It was almost as if the kidnappers knew their every move, but how? The leader was back in town...

Or was he?

Her stomach turned into knots over the thoughts forming in her head. How well did she really know Gunner? They'd only met a few days ago, and he was a very private, guarded person. The more she thought about it, the more she realized he'd been around during every questionable incident that had happened to her.

He'd had access to her backpack in the hotel the night he'd come in for a drink and turned her down for sex. He could have planted the note before he left to scare her off. He had also been in the community center at the time that someone had tried to kill her. He could have snuck into the storage room and pushed the shelves over on her.

How convenient that he had been the one to find her.

His hot and cold behavior toward her would explain a few things if he were the leader. Have sex with her so she would let her guard down, and then barely speak to her the next morning because he was concocting his evil plan. He could be taking every opportunity to get word to his men to try to kill her without looking guilty himself.

Her thoughts were running away with her as fast as the snowmobile they were on. She didn't want to believe the things she was thinking. He seemed so honorable and good, and she had developed genuine feelings for him. She could have sworn she saw glimpses of his feelings for her, but then he was so good at putting his walls back up and shutting her out.

She didn't know what to think.

Why didn't he bring her back to town with the others after this latest near death miss unless he had an ulterior motive? What could he possibly want from Astrid? Was he planning on getting rid of Emma and taking the girl himself to complete whatever mission he was on? Emma would have to play along because she didn't stand a chance of defending herself against someone like him.

He slowed the sled to a stop behind some bushes, and Emma's heart jumped into her throat. What was he going to do to her? He climbed off the sled and took off his helmet at the same time as her, then he gave her a funny look.

"You okay?"

"Fine. Just a little nausea. That was a bumpy ride. Why did we stop?"

He reached in his pack, and she jumped back, letting out a little squeak. Looking up at her with raised brows, he slowly handed her a piece of gum.

"Here. Chew this. It will help ease your stomach."

"Thanks." It might help ease her stomach, but it would do nothing to ease her nerves. "Sorry, I'm just on edge."

"Understandable. That death trap was meant for us."

"You don't seem to be on edge." She watched him carefully, looking for any sign that she might be wrong about him, but he wasn't giving her much hope.

He didn't meet her eyes as he fastened his pack and put it on. "One of us has to keep our cool." He stood up. "Let's go."

"Where are we going?"

"According to your map, the next cabin is up ahead. If one of them is that bad off, he'll probably still be there. Which means the other guy is the one sabotaging us. Maybe he'll double back to check on his trap and see that someone was injured. We might get lucky, and he'll assume we left to get help. The element of surprise is all we have in our favor. If we find the cabin, maybe we'll find the girl. It's worth a shot."

Or maybe he was luring Emma to her own death trap.

He talked a good game, saying all the right things, but wasn't that the point? Keep her off her guard? Pushing her thoughts to the back of her mind, she had no choice but to follow him. They hadn't gone very far before a gunshot went off.

Gunner dove at her, tackling her to the ground and laying on top of her just as the bullet whizzed past her head and hit a tree. She tapped his arm like a wrestler bowing out, and he rolled off her but held his finger up in a *shhhh* sign. Catching her breath, she tried to block out the fear of dying.

Why would he save her if he'd ordered someone to kill her?

He lifted his head slowly and searched the area with his gaze. He pulled out his gun and pointed to another tree, motioning for her to run. Confused and having no choice but to trust him, she did as he suggested and ran as fast as she could through the deep snow while he gave her cover by shooting in the direction the bullet had come from.

They ran from tree to tree, dodging and weaving, until they got too close to the edge of a hill and slid down. Gunner somehow reached out and grabbed her arm so they landed together halfway down the hill, breathing heavy and staring into each other's eyes.

Suddenly, one last gunshot went off and an avalanche of snow barreled down the hill right toward them. Fear gripped her like it had when she'd fallen beneath the ice and had thought she was going to drown. She stared up at the oncoming avalanche. There was no time to run. She didn't know which would be worse.

Drowning or being buried alive?

"Emma, listen to me." Gunner shook her until she looked at him. "I need you to stay focused. Make swimming motions uphill if you can, to keep your body toward the top of the snow as it carries us down the hill," Gunner quickly spoke.

"Okay." She nodded, trying not to hyperventilate.

"If you do start to go under, stick your hand up so you know which is the way out. It's easy to get disoriented, just like when you're hit with a big wave. Then make a pocket of air to breathe in. That will last you for thirty minutes."

"Pocket of air." She nodded, trying to remember everything.

He kissed her quickly on the lips. "Don't worry. I *will* find you," was the last thing he said to her before the snow swept them up like a tornado, tossing them about as it rolled down the hill.

* * *

"You dumbass. Don't you ever do anything stupid like that again," JoJo said to Harvey as he lay in his hospital bed with his bandaged leg hoisted in the air.

The smell of antiseptic assaulted her nose and turned her stomach. She hated hospitals. Ever since her mamaw faded away in one. JoJo, who was named after her and like her in every way, sat by her bedside every day for months. Her parents had both passed away when she was a teenager and her brother was off to college, so that left her.

Mamaw had been like a mother to her, and she'd lost her.

Harv was her rock, and she was terrified she was going to lose him.

Mr. Tall, Dark, and Dependable. She couldn't imagine life without him. Ever since her brother had first brought him home from college for a visit years ago, she'd felt this connection to him. When they became the Dream Team, she figured it was meant to be.

They were destined to be best friends.

He'd seen her through the loss of family members, the heartache of a breakup, the happiness of achieving her goals. He meant more to her than anyone she knew. Even her brother if she were being honest. They were inseparable.

What the hell would she do if she ever lost him?

Jack had left the hospital to brief the sheriff on everything that had gone down, and to rally a search and rescue team to go after Emma, Gunner, and Astrid. He was not happy that Gunner and Emma hadn't come back with Jack, Harv, and JoJo, given everything that had happened.

Now that the storm was over, the Cove had sustained considerable damage and would need every able body to help in the cleanup efforts. Abandoned cars needed towing. The local businesses needed repairs.

Snow removal was a problem since they didn't have any place to put it. And the marina had taken the hardest hit.

Speaking of able bodies. JoJo hadn't left the hospital since they'd arrived, and Harvey had been whisked off to surgery to remove the spear and stitch the torn muscles. He still looked larger than life to her, but she hated seeing him weak and vulnerable. He was finally awake, and she was mad as hell.

"Nice to see you, too, Trainwreck." He finally responded to her comment about not doing anything stupid ever again.

He'd never called her JoJo Coletrain. It was either Jo or Trainwreck. She gave him a hard time about it, but she secretly thought it was cute. But then she remembered where she was and what he'd just put her through.

She scowled. "What were you thinking? You might look like Goliath, but we both know you're more of a David."

"Maybe I wanted you to see me as Goliath for once." He locked his intelligent big brown eyes on hers, and she couldn't look away.

"Now why would you go and do a dumb thing like that?" He wasn't making any sense. Maybe he had a concussion.

"I don't know what I was thinking. I guess I wasn't."

"Exactly." She stabbed a finger in his direction. "You *always* overthink things. Leaping through the snow like some crazy ass fool and taking a nosedive into a pit over a flipping hat is so unlike you. I don't get it."

"You certainly 'got' everything Mr. Jack-of-all-Trades was doing." Harvey sighed and closed his eyes.

JoJo blinked.

"I guess I was jealous," he said softly, his lips tipping up a little. "I wanted to impress you."

"Why are men so ridiculous?" She grabbed her hair and pulled.

He shrugged. "Why are women so confusing?" He scratched his head.

Taking a deep breath, she let go of her fear. How bad could this be? Nothing could be worse than losing him. She decided to just go for it. What did she have to lose? She sat on the edge of Harvey's bed and reached out to take his hands in her own.

His eyes met hers.

"Look, Jack is cool. I like Jack, but you're my hero." She smiled tenderly, letting everything she felt show in her eyes. "I like you as David. You're quiet and smart and steady and clever. I'm loud and impulsive and reckless and, let's face it, a little bit crazy."

He laughed but didn't disagree.

"I can live with that, but if this relationship is going to work, we need for at least one of us to stay sane."

His smile dimmed, replaced by a wary look. "Relationship?" He swallowed hard.

"Yes, you big scaredy cat. I've had my heart set on you for a long time now, but I knew you were by-the-book and would never date a coworker. But don't you see, Harv? You're not just my coworker. You're my best friend. My soulmate. My freaking destiny, so buck up and get used to it, cuz it's happening."

"It is?" The first glimmer of hope filled his eyes.

"Hell yeah, it is." She leaned down and kissed him square on the mouth. To her surprise, he pulled her onto the bed with him, not seeming weak in the least, and kissed her until stars swam before her eyes.

Maybe a little bit of Goliath wasn't so bad after all.

* * *

Jack walked through the door of the community center. The storm was over and most people had gone back to their homes to start the cleanup, but he knew the sheriff was still using it as headquarters for the emergency.

Trent stood on the stage, speaking into a microphone. "Listen, folks, you have to be patient. We're doing the best we can. Power has been restored but the extent of the damage still has to be assessed. We're working as quickly as we can to help everyone out. Leave a list of your needs with my deputies, and we'll get to you as fast as we can."

"What about my daughter?" Haanes asked, pointing to his wife. "My poor, Carina, is beside herself with worry over Astrid."

The woman looked like she was on some heavy medication, if you asked Jack.

"Meanwhile, Clark Ford has all but disappeared with his daughter Mandy, and his wife's not talking." Haanes slammed his hand down on the table. "That's guilty behavior right there. What are you going to do about it, Sheriff?"

"He didn't disappear. Everyone's trying to get their lives back in order," one ski parent said. "Maybe you should do the same. I heard your check bounced when paying your daughter's last tuition bill."

"My affairs are none of your damn business. Maybe Ford needs to check on his wife. She seems to be MIA lately, too."

"Last I heard, Bart was helping her with her generator," another parent said. "You two fighting all the time isn't good for any of our girls."

"Look, his daughter needs him right now," someone else said.

"Exactly. My daughter needs me, too, but no one is helping me."

"That's not true. We're putting together a search and rescue team as we speak," Trent said.

"I don't hold out much hope, given how the last rescue attempt went," Haanes muttered, looking disheveled and unkempt. "I give up." He sat down next to his wife and stared off lifelessly.

Trent turned the microphone over to the mayor.

Laura's smile was full of compassion and hope. She was a petite thing, but she knew how to get the job done. Everyone in town trusted her. "Hang in there, folks. Coldwater Cove is resilient. We've survived other storms. We'll survive this, too. And rest assured our town is tough. The people are there for each other and always willing to help. We will get through this. I just know it. Thank you everyone. We'll reconvene tomorrow with more updates."

The sheriff made a beeline straight for Jack the second the mayor set the microphone down. "What the hell happened, Jack?"

"We almost died, that's what happened." Jack rubbed the back of his aching neck. "I don't know how, but these kidnappers knew we were coming. These guys aren't amateurs. They had explosives and blew a hole in the ice. Emma fell through for Christ's sake. She nearly drowned. Then they created a death trap meant for her. God only knows what they have planned next. Harvey's lucky to be alive, and now they probably know more people are looking for them. They're set on stopping whoever is following them."

"Then why the hell are Emma and Gunner still out there?"

"I know my sister. She's not going to stop until she rescues Astrid. Not after what happened to our sister." Jack clenched his jaw until his molars ached. "What I don't understand is why in the hell did Gunner Nash go along with it?"

14

GUNNER OPENED his eyes to blackness. He was beneath the snow, but he wasn't sure how deep. He dug a hole around his mouth for air. He spit and his saliva dribbled down his chin instead of up his face. He breathed out a sigh of relief.

Gravity.

That meant he was right side up. Wiggling, he managed to slip his arms out of his pack and unclip the small collapsible shovel he always carried with him. Digging upward, he slowly but surely made his way to the top and finally broke through the surface. His swimming motions had paid off, and he wasn't that far beneath the snow.

Closing his eyes for a moment, he prayed Emma had done the same.

It took a great deal of effort, but he finally managed to free himself. He looked around the area, hoping and praying for a sign. Something to show she was still alive. Nothing. He kept moving and looking little by little as he painstakingly made his way down the hill.

Gunner couldn't quite figure Emma Ross out. One minute she was making passionate love to him, to the point where he was freaked out because she made him feel things he hadn't felt in years, and that scared the hell out of him. So, he kept trying to distance himself physically, but that didn't mean she wasn't on his mind constantly. Being mentally distracted was going to get them both killed. Then today she'd kept looking at him like she didn't recognize him. She was skittish and jumpy and almost acted like she was afraid of him. It killed him that she might honestly think he would be capable of hurting a single hair on her precious body.

He should have listened to Jack.

He should have forced her to go with him back to the community center and get help. How lucky could they keep getting? One of these times, the kidnappers were going to succeed. Images of the woman and child he'd failed to rescue had haunted him to the point where he couldn't quit this mission.

He had to save that girl at any cost.

He closed his eyes for a moment, realizing the cost just might be his beguiling storm chaser. He shook his head, refusing to believe that was a possibility. His heart pinched, and he couldn't breathe. He'd never had a panic attack in his life until he met Emma.

He wasn't the praying kind, but he prayed for her sister to save her one more time. Suddenly a calm, warm, comforting feeling surrounded him like a hug. Opening his eyes, he looked around a little warily, then heard a noise from the sky.

A bald eagle circled overhead.

He was shocked. Bald eagles hibernated deep in their nests or in caves during the winter and emerged in the spring with their babies. What on earth was it doing in the sky after the nor'easter they just had?

When he looked back to the hill he was on, he sucked in a breath. A small speck of red poked out of the snow off to the left. Hope surged through his body. The side of an avalanche was the shallowest and moved the slowest. Lumbering the best he could to the side of the hill, he came to a stop then dropped to his knees.

Emma's red mitten.

She'd done what he'd told her to and put her hand up when she went under. He just had to hope she was still alive. He looked up to the sky, but the eagle was gone. He smiled slightly as he whispered, "Thank you, Ellie."

* * *

BLACKNESS SURROUNDED HER. Emma had never been claustrophobic but being buried alive in the snow was a new experience for her. She'd never been more terrified in her life than when Gunner had kissed her lips moments before the snow swept over them both and whisked them away.

She'd lost sight of him. She had a moment of panic, feeling as if it was a goodbye kiss, and she would never see him again. Then she remembered what he said, and she focused. His words were the only thing that kept her going. She visualized everything he told her to do and started swimming uphill.

Now she knew how salmon must feel swimming upstream because she felt like she was getting nowhere. It felt weird and seemed crazy to try to swim through snow against gravity, but he had told her it would keep her at the top of the avalanche. So, she swam hard and fast, thrashing her arms and legs about.

The snow had been relentless, tossing her about as if she were in a washing machine. She'd once been tossed about like that in the ocean by a rogue wave. It had disoriented her and had made it difficult for her to figure out which way was up.

Eventually she felt the sand beneath her and began to crawl toward the shore based on the direction of the wave above her. That had rattled her, making her not go back in the ocean for quite some time. She didn't have sand to guide her, so she struggled in the direction away from how the snow was rolling. It was exhausting.

Storms she could handle. She knew how to predict the weather and stay out of the storm's direct path, getting close enough to do her research, and then retreating to safety until the storm passed. She knew better. The fact that it was a teenage girl in a nor'easter at risk of dying like her sister had made her think irrationally.

Emma couldn't withstand such agonizing pain again.

She couldn't survive again at someone else's expense. The difference this time was that it wasn't just a girl lost in a storm. Astrid had been kidnapped by ruthless men. Men who wanted anyone who was foolish enough to follow them dead.

But why?

Emma now knew there was no way Gunner was involved. He'd been shot at along with her and caught in the same avalanche. He wouldn't have put himself in harm's way if he were the leader. For all she knew he could be dead.

The thought that she never got to tell him how he made her feel would haunt her forever if he died. She wasn't afraid to die. She faced danger all the time in her line of work. She was afraid to live. But after falling through the ice and having her sister guide her to safety, she knew she was meant to live and be happy.

She carried her sister's strength with her now.

Gunner had been the first person to make her feel alive. How ironic that she might lose everything after finally finding happiness. The only good thing about being buried in snow was that she wasn't cold anymore. Harvey would give her a lecture if he knew, and JoJo would flat out yell at her. Jack? Well, Jack would just be disappointed in her, and that bothered her the most.

"Emma!"

Emma held her breath.

"Emma, can you hear me? Wiggle your hand if you can."

Gunner.

Tears started running down Emma's face. She wasn't sure if it was because she was getting rescued or the fact that Gunner was alive. Her arm and hand were numb, but she managed to move her fingers. At least she hoped she did.

"Oh, thank God. That's it, baby. I've got you. Hang tight."

What seemed like forever was probably only a few moments. Finally, he scooped the snow away from her head. His face was mere inches away from hers.

"Hi," he said softly.

"Hi." She laughed, and then the tears started to fall harder.

He kissed her lips gently and then got to work digging her out. She'd never been through anything so scary in her life.

"Thank the Lord you found me," she said.

"Thank your sister." He kept digging.

"My sister?" Was he kidding?

"I know what you're thinking, and no, I'm not crazy." He looked so serious, and sincerity rang through his voice. "I prayed and asked her for help. I felt her this time, too, and then I saw an eagle."

"An eagle." Emma looked at him with raised eyebrows.

"I know. They hibernate, but I wasn't hallucinating. I saw an eagle and after that, I saw your red glove."

Emma gasped, staring at him in awe, her eyes glistening with unshed tears. "Wow, my sister saved me again."

"Well, I am doing *my* part I'd say. And *you* definitely did everything right." He winked, and then helped her out of the hole just in time.

A noise from up the hill sounded.

"We should get going." He grabbed his pack and put it back on, then led the way into the woods.

"You don't have to tell me twice." She quickly followed. "I don't want to get caught in another avalanche."

"That, and I don't care to get shot at again."

Her gaze raised to the ridge above one last time before she disappeared into the woods behind him. "You think someone is still up there?"

"I think someone won't stop hunting us until they get their kill. At this point we don't even know if Astrid is still alive."

"We need to get to that cabin. I'm sure she's there with the guy who's injured." Emma kept pace with him as they moved deeper into the woods where they had at least some protection.

"Maybe, but we have to get around the man hunting us."

It took a while, but they finally made their way back up the hill, stopping and listening and watching for an ambush along the way. Emma felt guilty. She wanted to come clean about the leader, but first, she wanted to explain why she was so set on rescuing Astrid.

Nearly dying had a way of changing a person.

"You know how I mentioned I had a twin sister who died in a nor'easter like this one?" Emma paused.

He eyed her curiously and nodded as they walked side-by-side.

"What you don't know is the whole story. Ellie was

my other half," Emma finally continued. "We did everything together. We looked identical and were inseparable, but we were so different. Ellie played it safe and second guessed everything. I was the impulsive adventurous one." Emma saw a ray of sunshine stream through the trees to guide their way on the forest floor and thought of her sister.

She was starting to realize Ellie was her guardian angel and with her always.

"Ellie was the first born. Even though we were only five minutes apart, she took that roll to heart." Emma smiled. "She was an old soul and acted more like a parent, always looking out for me. She didn't want to go cross country skiing that day, but I refused to listen to her." Emma's face pinched and she pressed her lips together for a moment, finding it hard to speak before looking at Gunner.

He remained quiet and patient, listening to her every word.

"There was a weather watch for a possible nor'easter that day, but I didn't care much about the weather back then and I never watched the news. Ellie watched every broadcast. She wanted to be a journalist when we graduated high school and went to college in the fall. I had no clue what I wanted to be at that time." Emma swallowed past the lump in her throat, fighting back tears.

"It's okay," he said softly. "You don't have to tell me."

"I was selfish as usual," She kept talking, lost in her memories. "There was a blanket of fresh snow. I wanted to go cross country skiing and didn't believe we were in any real danger. When I wouldn't listen to her warnings, she followed me, refusing to let me go skiing alone. That was Ellie. Always willing to be the one to sacrifice."

"She sounds like a special woman."

"She was. At first, everything was great. We had made it to the trail way out in the woods and were having a great time." Emma looked off into the distance, remembering. "That was when the storm hit with a vengeance. We tried to outrun it and make our way back to town, but the snow was falling at a fast, heavy rate. The winds picked up, and the visibility got worse." Emma couldn't speak for a moment, the pain as fresh this moment as if it had just happened rather than years ago.

He reached out and held her hand. She squeezed tight and didn't let go.

"I was a better skier than Ellie. I was going too fast for her to keep up. She yelled for me to wait, and I hollered back for her to speed up. I just wanted to escape the storm before we couldn't see anymore. Panic drove me to ski even faster. I honestly thought she was right behind me. By the time I reached the edge of town, I could barely see. The whiteout conditions made it so you couldn't see more than ten feet." A sob slipped past Emma's lips. "When I turned around, Ellie was gone. I made it to the community center and tried to get help, but no one would listen, just like this time."

"You wanted to go back for her, didn't you?" His tone was filled with sympathy and understanding.

"I tried, but my parents wouldn't let me. Jack was so angry. He tried to go back for her, too, but they wouldn't let him, either. They were devastated, but they wouldn't risk losing all of us. We had to wait in agony until the storm was over, and then the entire town went out and searched for her, but it was too late." Emma shook her head back and forth.

Gunner tightened his hand around hers, and she felt his strength.

"They found her way off the trail, frozen to death on the lake where I was shot. She must have been looking for that first cabin, but didn't make it. I'll never forgive myself. I should have stopped when she yelled at me to wait for her, but I panicked. I didn't know she'd fallen that far back. I thought she could catch up to me." Emma looked at Gunner with all the pain she felt on full display. "I left my own sister out there to die."

Gunner pulled her into his arms and held her while she cried. He didn't say a word, just held her tight while she let it all out. He had no idea how much that meant to her. He didn't try to make her feel better or fix anything, he just listened.

When they finally broke apart, she wiped her eyes. "Thank you."

"You're not alone, you know," he finally said as they started walking again. "My best friend, Max, and I went into the Navy Seals together. He was like a brother to me. We felt incredible after surviving Hell Week and making the same team."

"*He* sounds like a special person."

"He *was* special." Gunner frowned. "Coming from a long line of military family members, I felt such pride and honor to serve my country and help others. Max didn't have a family. He was an orphan, in and out of foster care with people who didn't give a crap about him. We met during our senior year of high school and became best friends. I talked him into following my path, and he gladly did. We went on so many missions together. Did so many great things, but the job was getting to him. I could tell."

"What happened?"

"Just before we went on our last mission, he confessed to me that he'd gotten hooked on drugs to ease his anxiety and depression. He said he was sorry and that he loved me like a brother. It felt strange, almost like a goodbye. Like he was giving up. I promised to help him when the mission was over." A muscle in Gunner's jaw bulged as he clenched his teeth and breathed deeply through his nose.

Emma touched his arm. "It's okay."

He stared at her hand on his arm. "We were on a rescue mission in Mexico to save an innocent woman and her child from the cartel. Everything was going according to plan. We almost had them to safety, when Max backed out of the room and the rest of us were ambushed. My entire team, including the woman and child, were killed. I was the only one who made it out alive."

"What happened to Max?"

"He traded us all in exchange for drugs. He knew we were going to be ambushed, but he kept that information to himself and set us all up. He set *me* up. I don't know how he could do something like that to me. His brother." Gunner's gaze locked onto Emma's, filled with anguish and heartbreak for a brief moment before being schooled behind a blank expression once more. "I've never trusted anyone not to lie to me since then." His eyes softened. "Until you."

"Gunner, there's something I have to tell you. I—"

A bullet rang through the air and hit Emma's backpack, making her stumble, her words lost in the moment.

15

GUNNER PULLED Emma to her feet and they ran. Zigzagging though the woods, he spotted a cluster of brush against a small hill that didn't look out of the ordinary at first glance. Growing closer to inspect it, he realized it covered the opening of a small cave. He covered their tracks with a branch then made a shushing sign at Emma, and they ducked inside. He pulled the brush over the opening and sat back to wait.

He quietly pulled out his gun when they heard footsteps outside. The footsteps stopped for a moment, then walked around in a circle several times. The man cursed, then finally moved on. Gunner let out the breath he'd been holding.

They'd made it.

He could kick himself for losing focus while they bonded over stories. He understood her better after hearing her story, and he'd never opened up like that to anyone, but he knew better. This was not the time or place for that.

"That was scary." Emma took off her pack to rest for a minute.

A thought occurred to Gunner. "Let me see that." He reached for her pack, and she handed it to him.

"We stayed well off the trail. I don't get how the kidnapper always seems to know exactly where we are."

He examined the bullet hole and then unzipped her bag. This guy who was chasing them was a pro, but no one was that good. Gunner pulled all her equipment out, looking over each piece. He arched a brow at her hunting knife and set it aside.

She rolled her eyes.

When the bag was empty, he examined the bag itself. Searching every nook and cranny of the material. His hand paused, his gaze looking up and meeting hers as he pulled out a small device wedged into an inside pocket.

"What's that?" she asked. "I've never seen that before." He studied her eyes but only saw honest sincerity and puzzlement.

"A tracking device," he said, point blank, and then smashed it.

"What?" She gaped. "Who could have put that in there?"

"Good question." He thought about it. "It had to be someone back in town before you left."

She stared at her pack but didn't say anything.

"Emma, those guys aren't working alone," he went on. "That certainly explains how the kidnappers have been one step ahead of us at all times. Who from town would want to kidnap the girl, and why?"

"Now that they can't track us, they might be in a hurry to move Astrid from the cabin. We should go." Emma refilled her pack and then stood. "We've come this far. We can't go back now."

Gunner stood and grabbed his own pack, wanting to reassure her. "Don't worry. We won't leave the girl behind."

After everything Emma had gone through, he understood she would do just about anything to save this girl. Now someone would do anything to stop her. She had no way of knowing that someone would track her every move. That had to terrify her.

"At least without the tracker, we have the upper hand."

This time they were behind the kidnapper, so they could turn the tables on the hunter and track him. Let them see what it felt like to be hunted. Once they found the girl, they would double back and retrieve the sled. He felt better that they had a plan. It didn't take long to pick up the trail. They moved swiftly, keeping out of sight. They were getting close to dusk when they finally found the cabin.

The sound of raised voices came from inside.

"What do you mean, you don't know where they are, Nikolai?" came a male voice. "Boss put a tracking device in the woman's pack."

"No shit, Boris. But one minute I was following the signal, and the next it stopped," said the other man who must be Nikolai.

"Boss isn't going to like that."

"I don't care. I'm done taking orders. We need to finish the mission and not worry if they're still alive or not."

The sound of a commotion happened, and Emma and Gunner moved close enough to see in the window, staying just out of sight.

"Shit. Get the girl. Don't let her get away." Boris sat on a bed, rebandaging his leg. "I'll be ready to go in a minute."

Nikolai grabbed the girl by her arm just as she opened the door. He yanked her back inside and kicked it closed. "You're not going anywhere, princess."

"I hate you!" she screamed. "My father will ruin you when he finds you."

"Your father's a pussy."

"Shut up." She slapped him across the face.

"I'll shut you up for good if you try that again." He slapped her harder, and she cried out in pain.

Emma stood.

Gunner pulled her down beside him.

"What was that?" Boris stared out the window.

"What are you talking about?" Nikolai tied a crying Astrid's hands in front of her and shoved her down on a chair.

"I saw something. Right out there." He pointed out the window.

Emma and Gunner were about fifteen feet away, hunched behind some bushes, holding their breath.

"I don't see anything." Nikolai squinted through the window.

Boris grabbed his gun. "Check it out before we leave anyway. I don't want to take any chances."

"I told you, I'm done taking orders from anyone." He stared at Astrid. "Maybe it's time we forget Boss's plan and make one of our own."

Gunner took off his pack and pulled out his gun and survival knife as he whispered to Emma, "Wait until I'm around the side of the cabin, and then throw this rock at the window."

"Okay." She touched his arm, looking afraid yet brave, and breathtakingly beautiful to him. "Be careful."

He nodded, kissed her lips, and then sprinted around the cabin.

* * *

EMMA SUCKED IN A BREATH, worried sick. She knew he was a Navy Seal, but it was still scary having him take on a killer by himself. These men had proven they were ruthless. She'd been through so much with Gunner. He couldn't die before she had a chance to tell him how she felt.

She should have come clean about knowing there was a mole after her from the beginning, but at that time, she didn't know who she could trust. Now she realized she should have shown him the note threatening her to back off. He'd deserved to hear it from her.

He was going to hate her for knowingly putting them in danger.

"There it is again," Boris said. "I saw a flash of something."

"It's probably just an animal."

Shoot. She was supposed to be paying attention. Emma shook off her distraction and threw the rock hard. It hit the cabin wall right by the window.

Nikolai grabbed his gun and walked out the front door. He scanned the trees but instead of heading in the direction of the sound so Gunner could jump him, he twisted around and got the jump on Gunner.

All hell broke loose.

Astrid screamed and ran out of the cabin. Boris hobbled out the door and shot at Astrid. Gunner and Nikolai wrestled on the ground, struggling with a knife. No one paid any attention to Emma.

She scrambled over to Gunner and grabbed his gun, backing up several steps. She raised her hand and pointed the gun at the pair, but they were a twisting mass of arms and limbs. She was terrified she would shoot the wrong man.

Nikolai held the knife at Gunner's throat, nicking his flesh. Emma's hand shook as she aimed the gun at Nikolai's back. Gunner saw the look on her face, and a surge of strength came over him. He flipped Nikolai over and impaled the knife in the man's chest.

Nikolai's face transformed to one of shock and disbelief before the life faded out of him. Gunner rolled to his feet and slowly walked over to Emma. He took the gun from her trembling fingers and pulled her in for a hug.

"It's over now," he whispered into her hair.

"Not so fast. Drop the gun or the girl dies." Boris emerged from the woods, holding a gun to a bruised and bloody Astrid's head.

Gunner had whipped the gun up and stepped in front of Emma, pointing it at Boris as soon as he'd appeared in his line of fire. He kept the gun raised, studying him.

"Please don't let him kill me," Astrid cried.

"Shut up!" Boris jammed his gun against her temple. "You're more trouble than you're worth."

"Easy," Gunner said with a deadly tone Emma had never heard. "You shoot the girl, I shoot you."

Boris looked at Emma. "And you! Boss warned you not to go after the girl. But you had to tell everyone and do it anyway."

Gunner flinched as if someone had hit him but kept the gun on Boris. "What's he talking about?"

"I'll explain later." Emma stepped out from behind him and held her head high, staring at Boris. "I didn't tell anyone anything. I came alone. I can't help it people followed me." She couldn't look at Gunner but she felt his eyes burning into her.

"You weren't supposed to come at all, you stupid bitch. You've ruined everything," Boris sneered, his face transforming into a monster's.

"You knew they were working with someone in town?" Gunner asked in disbelief. "You knew we could be walking into a trap and you didn't tell me? After everything I told you about my past, you still didn't tell me?"

"I received a threatening note to back off and that if

I told anyone, they would kill the girl," she tried to explain. "I had no choice."

"Everyone has a choice," Gunner's tone changed. "You purposely put us in harm's way. Did you know about the tracking device too?"

"No." Her heart was breaking, and she wanted to cry, but she held herself together for Astrid's sake. "You have to believe me."

He didn't answer, instead giving her a look that said this is no time for a lovers' quarrel. They needed to look like a united front. Boris shuffled his feet and Gunner snapped to attention, retraining his gun on Boris's head.

"Astrid, you're going to be okay, honey, you can do this. Remember your training," Emma said until the girl focused on her. Emma needed her to understand what she wanted her to do. That was the only thing holding Emma together right then.

"Stop talking to the girl," Boris growled, a bead of sweat rolling down his temple. He yanked Astrid closer to him.

"How can you be so cruel. I'm just trying to mentally prepare her for what's about to happen." Emma stared into Astrid's eyes, trying to get her to understand her meaning by using words she'd heard the coaches use with the other girls. "You know, like when you're in a race and need to be in the right position?"

Astrid stared at her as dawning filled her eyes.

"You're talking nonsense," Boris said. "What's about to happen is you're going to go fetch that snowmobile of yours, and I'm taking the girl out of here myself. You'll pay for killing my partner."

"That's not likely. I'm an expert marksman. Can you say the same?" Gunner narrowed his eyes. "Who's your boss?"

Boris's eyes widened in surprise for a moment, but

then they narrowed to slits. "I'll die before I tell you." He sneered.

"That can be arranged," Gunner replied calmly, which was far more intimidating, then tipped his head to the side and cracked his neck as he adjusted his aim.

"Astrid, look at me," Emma said. "I want you to get into position."

"Shut up!" Boris cocked his gun.

"Tuck!" Emma yelled.

Astrid dropped into a downhill skier's stance, bending her knees and tucking.

Gunner pulled the trigger.

* * *

No! No! No! No!

Fuck no!

The streets were full of way too many cops and the rumor mill was buzzing.

When Jack Ross came back with the wounded Michelin Man and his pink flamingo, telling everyone the kidnappers were trying to kill them, the sheriff had called in surrounding law enforcement to aid in the search and rescue.

Nikolai had reassured me he would take them out at any cost. I should have taken care of the matter myself. He hadn't taken care of any one of them. The rescue teams had arrived back in town moments ago and headed straight to the hospital.

Every single fucking one of my loose ends was alive and back in Coldwater Cove.

They were getting debriefed. Everyone was waiting for word on what happened. The only thing we knew for sure was that both Boris and Nikolai were dead while Emma Ross, the Navy Seal and the girl were all still very much alive.

I had to find out if my men had talked.

A moment of panic twisted my gut. What if my men told someone who I was before they died? They were weak. What if that Navy Seal tortured it out of them.? I couldn't go to jail. I didn't want to run and make it look obvious. Because if the idiots didn't tell anyone who I was, then I could walk away relatively unscathed with no one the wiser.

But I would know.

I would have to go back to my old life. Fury filled me. Everything I'd worked so hard for had been for nothing. This plan had taken time and money, and that bitch had ruined everything. This deal would have changed my life.

I didn't know if I could let it go.

I fucking wanted to kill her with my bare hands. Wrap them around her throat and rip her vocal chords out. Maybe I would for the hell of it. Maybe no one would know. Maybe it was time to move on from the Cove.

And maybe, just maybe, I would get away with it.

16

GUNNER SAT in Trent's office with Emma and Jack, getting debriefed on everything that had happened. He hadn't said a word since that bombshell had been dropped on him. He was still processing everything that had happened. Astrid was at the hospital being treated for her injuries with her relieved parents. Meanwhile, Harvey was doing well recovering from his injuries with JoJo by his side.

Right after Gunner had pulled the trigger, law enforcement officers from various departments across the county had descended upon them. Boris died without revealing who the leader was. Same with Nikolai. All parties were escorted back to town and immediately whisked away.

Emma had been shot, had a concussion, nearly drowned beneath the ice, and had been buried beneath an avalanche yet she refused to go to the hospital, much to her parents' dismay. She insisted on going straight to the sheriff's office and telling what she knew.

Too little too late.

Now that they were safe, Gunner's emotions that had been simmering just beneath the surface were boiling over. Shock, disappointment, regret...anger. He felt betrayed by someone he cared about all over again. It hit too close to home for him. If she had told him everything she knew, he wouldn't have felt ambushed hearing it from someone else.

She could have gotten them all killed.

Yes, she wanted to save the girl. He did, too. But there was a right way and a dangerous way to go about it. Her recklessness wasn't good for anyone. He couldn't even look at her without feeling a deep sense of hurt all over again.

Whatever had started between them was over.

"Wait, tell me again when you received the threatening note." The sheriff jotted down notes as he sat behind his desk.

"After I was shot on the ice, Gunner rescued me and we came back to town. The storm was in full force at that time, so we were all at the community center. Someone must have heard me tell you what I saw and try to convince you to go after Astrid." Emma pulled a note out of her pocket and set it on the table. "Gunner took me back to the hotel. He came in for a drink and then left." She didn't make eye contact with him.

Gunner sat silently.

Jack frowned.

Emma continued, "Then the next morning, I was about to head back to the community center when I found this is my backpack."

BACK OFF, BITCH! STOP STICKING YOUR NOSE IN PLACES IT DOESN'T BELONG, OR NEXT TIME I'll SHOOT TO KILL! SHOW ANYONE THIS NOTE, AND THE GIRL DIES!

. . .

"No one else was in your room while your pack was there except Gunner, correct?" Trent asked.

"Correct. The only way someone could have put something in my pack was earlier when we were at the community center." Her gaze locked onto Gunner's and she sat up straight, refusing to look away first.

He finally broke the contact.

She added in a tone filled with emotion, "At one point, I thought maybe he was the leader behind the kidnapping."

That brought Gunner's attention back to her, but she was looking at Trent with her shoulders squared.

"He coincidentally was at the right time and place to rescue me several times," she went on. "He had access to my backpack in the hotel room. He conveniently was the one who found me in the storage room of the community center beneath the shelves. The kidnappers were always one step ahead of us, so I thought maybe he'd ordered them to set off the explosive to make me fall through the ice. When he didn't follow Jack, Harvey, and JoJo, I thought he might be leading me into a trap."

Jack whipped his head in Gunner's direction.

The sheriff's hand paused.

Gunner clenched his jaw, but didn't say a word or look away from Emma. He was used to being set up. He didn't expect this time to be any different, but he couldn't deny that her mistrust in him stung.

She sighed a little sadly and her shoulders slumped as she looked back at Trent and continued her story. "But then I realized Gunner couldn't be the leader. He wouldn't have ordered the avalanche to be set off, knowing he would be buried alive along with me. Then we found the tracking device in my backpack and realized the real leader must have put it in there again at the community center. I kept my promise and didn't tell anyone about the threatening note, hoping to buy some time as I kept trying to get people to help me look for Astrid before the storm ended and we lost her for good."

"We almost lost you all for good, Em." Jack shook his head.

Emma looked down at her lap. "And I'm sorry for that. I never meant to worry you. I was just doing what I felt was right."

Trent held up his hand for Jack to be silent. "Go ahead, Emma. What happened next?"

"After Gunner smashed the tracking device, we were able to make our way around the cabin without the kidnappers knowing for sure where we were." She looked back up at her brother and raised her chin a notch. "I was right. They were moving out. We got there just in time. I know I made a lot of mistakes," her gaze was full of sincerity and regret when it met Gunner's, "and I should have come clean regardless of the risk to Astrid, but I would do it all over again to save her. I will forever be grateful to you for your help."

Gunner looked away. He was relieved they hadn't lost another innocent victim, but he couldn't trust Emma and he didn't know if he ever would.

"Do you have anything to add, Mr. Nash?" The sheriff looked at him.

"No," was all he said. "What's the next step?"

"Trent figures out who ordered the kidnapping of Astrid and the hit on Emma and locks the son of a bitch up," Jack said through his clenched teeth, "or so help me God, Coldwater Cove will have another murder on its hands."

Gunner couldn't have said it better himself. He knew that look well, only he wasn't waiting around for the sheriff. He might be angry with Emma, but that didn't mean anyone else could touch one single hair on her head.

* * *

"I HATE that I can't help with the cleanup," Harvey said from his perch on a barstool at The Claw.

JoJo sat beside him, manning his crutches and watching his every move. "You aren't making a move unless I say so."

"Doctor's orders?" He pushed his glasses up his nose.

"JoJo's orders." She looked at him as if daring him to say otherwise. He didn't say a word. He just stared at her for a moment as his eyes softened, and then he winked at her until she blushed.

Harvey winked at JoJo, and she *blushed*.

"What is happening here." Emma looked back and forth between them, trying to process what she was seeing and hearing. "I don't understand."

JoJo leaned forward and planted a kiss on Harvey's lips. "Understand that?"

Harvey held JoJo's hand and grinned wide.

JoJo rolled her eyes but didn't let go.

"Obviously I missed a whole lot in a day." Emma took a big sip of her draft beer, her mind whirling, but she wasn't really all that surprised. Things happened fast in storms. Relationships formed and bonds intensified just like the weather. She thought of her own situation. Sometimes they fizzled out just as quickly.

"A near death experience will make you see things real clear." JoJo squared her shoulders. "This isn't going to be a problem, is it?"

"Not for me." Emma shrugged. "Friends or lovers, we're still a team."

"I'll drink to that." Harvey signaled the bartender.

"Not on my watch," JoJo said. "Painkillers, remember?"

"Which go great with milk." He ordered milk and a plate of Oreo cookies.

"What are you, five?" JoJo eyed the plate when the bartender set it down moments later. "You gonna share?"

"You know it." He slid the plate between them and handed her a cookie. "Anything for my girl."

"I like the sound of that." JoJo took the cookie and patted his hand.

"Want one?" Harvey asked Emma as an afterthought, not taking his gaze off JoJo. The two had eyes only for each other.

"I'm good." Emma chuckled and took another sip of her beer. Damn, it felt good to be back.

Jack had removed the boards from the windows the day the storm stopped and had begun to clean up the damage to the bar. Since the town all banded together to help, he'd opened his doors to anyone who wanted anything to eat or drink on him.

The Cove was good like that.

Always came together to help others in need, especially since the new sheriff and mayor had come into office. She was glad to see things were getting better in their small town, but there was still the fact that they had an evil person among them. And no matter where she went, she still felt eyes on her.

"Told you that storm was gonna come early," Eugene said before removing his cap and saluting Gunner.

"That you did." Gunner paused beside his stool. "You're not feeling any more bad weather, are you?"

"Nah. Smooth sailing from here on out." Eugene slapped his fishing hat back on his head and drank from his pint.

Gunner clapped him on the shoulder. "Good to hear, old man."

"Who you callin' old? Don't you worry yourself, son. I still got some spring in these arthritic bones." Eugene winked.

"I bet you do." Gunner laughed.

His smile slipped when his gaze met Emma's. He tipped his head at Harvey, JoJo, and her, then he kept moving until he reached her brother and father who were repairing some water damage in the front from the initial storm surge.

"What's happening here," JoJo threw Emma's words back at her, "I don't understand." She fluttered her eye lashes innocently.

"You and me both," Emma said on a sigh as her mother approached with Vanessa walking beside her.

"Let me check my book when I get back to my shop and see what I have available," Vanessa said to Emma's mother, Dori, but I'm sure I can find room to squeeze you in." She smiled at Emma. "Your hair still looks fabulous. In fact, I think this style suits your face better than the one you had before."

"Thanks again. I really appreciate you coming to my rescue." Emma touched the multi-layered look. "It's growing on me."

Vanessa peeked at JoJo, eying her hair with interest. "And you. I would love to get my hands on that funky hair of yours."

"Still not lettin' anyone touch my hair. I got her down to a science." JoJo ran a hand over her pink strands that looked like she'd just rolled out of bed.

"If you change your mind, you know where my shop is. Take care, ladies." Vanessa waved and left the pub, staring at Jack as she walked out the door.

"Such a nice girl. I think she's sweet on Jack,"

Emma's mother said with a little smile, then her gaze landed on Emma. "I think someone else is sweet on you."

"Maybe at one time, but not so much anymore." Emma looked over at Gunner.

He glanced back at her as if drawn to her as well, but then he quickly looked away.

Her mother wrapped her arms around her and held on tight. She'd been doing that from the moment Emma had emerged from the woods. Emma didn't complain. She was happy to see her family, too. Her job put her at risk a lot and she'd stayed away for far too long, but over the past few days there had been too many moments where she genuinely didn't think she would make it back alive.

"I'm still worried about you," her mother said when she finally pulled away. "No one knows why Astrid was kidnapped, which is scary enough. But the person who was calling the shots is still out there, and it's someone from our very own town. That's terrifying. Have you received any more notes?"

"No, nothing."

"Are you sure you're not just saying that so I won't worry."

"Yes, Mom." It was Emma's fault her own family was hesitant to believe her, but she was telling the truth. "I'm scared, too. Believe me, I want this person behind bars. I can't go through my life constantly looking over my shoulder. I'm hoping Sheriff West will find a lead soon."

But if she had to figure that out on her own, then so be it.

* * *

"THANK you for asking me to lunch," Emma said to Stacy the next day. "I love my family and they mean well, but I needed a break from all the smothering."

"I figured as much, and the Lost Horizon is one of the businesses that didn't sustain much damage from the storm. Harry was a big help bringing in food and especially desserts to the community center. The kids really needed a pick me up after the blizzard hit. This is one of their hangouts. He's always been fond of the local teenagers. Takes a lot of pictures of them for free. He's very generous."

"Really? I grew up with him, but I really didn't know him that well. He kept to himself a lot. Spent a lot of time in the woods taking pictures." Emma took a sip of her iced tea and a bite of her Ruben sandwich.

"He still does." Stacy gestured to the pictures hanging on the walls of his diner. She'd ordered a tuna melt and a lemonade.

"The food is delicious. Seems like Harry is doing well for himself these days. Do the kids up at the academy ever come into town and hang out here, too?"

"Sometimes. When they have down time. Usually on the weekends." She eyed Emma curiously. "I know what you're wondering, and you'd be right."

"What's that?"

"Astrid was the closest thing to a celebrity that we had around here, other than Vanessa during her Miss America days. All the kids love Harry, but not Astrid. She looked down her nose at him, like she did most people in town. Pretty much everyone just chalked it up to her being a foreigner and thinking she was better than them."

"Maybe it didn't sit well with Harry. After growing up pretty much isolated from others, he seems to be a town favorite now. At least with the kids. Maybe it was a blow to his ego when she shunned him, so he did something about it. Maybe he didn't want money. Maybe he just wanted to scare her. Teach her a lesson so that's why there was no ransom."

"Maybe," Stacy said and shrugged.

"Who knows? Maybe I'm just reaching." Emma shook her head. "I just hope we figure this out soon. I feel like I'm losing my mind. Everywhere I go, I feel eyes on me. Like someone is watching my every move, waiting to strike. It's unnerving."

"I know how you feel. It wasn't that long ago that I was looking into my mother's murder. People in this town don't like when someone makes waves. I didn't trust the police back then, but Trent is different. Word of advice," Stacy said with a gentle tone. "You'd do well to not interfere and let my husband do his job. I would hate to see anything more happen to you." Stacy reached out and squeezed Emma's hand. "Haven't you been through enough?"

They finished their lunch in a strained silence.

"Thank you again, Stacy. I really do appreciate it."

"You're welcome, and hey, I hope I didn't say anything to upset you. I just didn't want you to have to experience what I went through."

"No, you're right. I have been through enough." Emma stood. "I'd better get back and help my parents and brother at the pub. "See you around."

"Bye." Stacy waved as Emma walked out the door behind Harry with his camera equipment.

Stacy was right about one thing. Emma had been through enough. Emma watched Harry drive off toward the woods. After everything that had happened, she really shouldn't take matters into her own hands again. She hesitated for only a second, and then put her rental car in drive to follow him. It was Harry, after all.

He had never been a threat. She couldn't imagine he was now. Besides, she'd never had the patience to wait for backup, and she'd definitely been through *more* than enough.

Maybe it was time she did something about it.

17

"You wanted to see me?" Gunner asked the mayor, Laura Baker-Flemming, as he stood in her office doorway in the Town Hall and looked around. The walls were covered with pictures of all the work her office had accomplished around town. Stacey's mother would be proud.

"Ah, yes, Mr. Nash." Laura smiled wide. "Have a seat."

She was a petite blonde, who most people underestimated, but he had seen her in action. She was fair but firm, with a no-tolerance policy for crimes committed in her town. She shuffled a stack of papers on her desk and then looked up at him.

"Please, call me Gunner." He sat in a chair across from her desk.

"Then you should definitely call me Laura."

"Done." He nodded. "What can I help you with?"

She stood and closed her office door then returned to her seat. "I normally wouldn't involve just anyone in a mayoral matter, but given the situation, my hands are tied." She scanned her notes. "Haanes Westergaard understandably wants answers on who the men who kidnapped his daughter were."

"What father wouldn't?"

"Exactly. My office did some digging, but he didn't like what we found. Haanes is a Scandinavian diplomat from Sweden who often visits the United States on official business, other than just his daughter's ski career."

"Don't they have ski academies in his country?"

"Apparently, they're very competitive. His daughter stands out more in America, but that doesn't sit well with the locals."

"I can imagine he's made a few enemies along the way."

"You have no idea. Meanwhile, he unfortunately got linked to some questionable business people here in the U.S. involving criminal acts, but because of Diplomatic Immunity, we can't touch him. Most countries frown on prosecuting foreign officials in hopes of maintaining good relations between the countries. That's where you come in."

"How so?"

"Haanes isn't talking. He might want answers, but not at the expense of his reputation. He still believes Clark Ford hired the kidnappers to take his daughter out of the ski competitions so Ford's daughter would move up the ranks. Haanes won't give us any information on the people he was working with, denying any involvement. I think he might be in financial trouble with them, which would explain his check bouncing for Astrid's tuition. From what I gather, these people are not the kind you cross."

"I've met a few of those." Memories of the cartel tried to surface, but Gunner pushed them down.

"I bet you have." She studied him closer. "And that's why I think you're exactly what this town needs."

"I'm listening."

"To be honest, I don't care about Haanes Westergaard's international affairs. I care about Coldwater

Cove. I want to know if Boris and Nikolai—if those are even their real names—were related to the scandal Haanes is involved in. Were they after his daughter to get back whatever Haanes took from their boss or maybe as payback to teach him a lesson? If we can find out how the kidnappers are linked to Haanes, then maybe we can find out who they were working for. I don't like the idea that we still have a dangerous puppet master walking our streets."

"What do you want me to do?"

"You're still a Navy Seal, correct?"

"Yes."

"Then you must have contacts who can help you in situations like this. I know it's a big ask, given his immunity, but maybe you know someone who can look into the identities of these men off the books."

"I know some people. I'll see what I can find out."

"Thank you. I really appreciate this. I just want the streets of this town to be safe. If I can do anything for you, just say the word."

"You're welcome." He stood to leave, then thought of something else and looked back at Laura. "What about Haanes's wife, Carina? She's married to the man. Maybe she's heard something."

"I already tried." Laura sighed. "Unfortunately, the poor woman needs help. It was clear while talking with her that she's addicted to drugs. My sources say she was in a car crash a year ago that nearly killed her and was on some pretty heavy pain meds after that. I don't know what she's on now, but she clearly has a problem."

"How's Astrid holding up through all of this?"

"She just wants to go home. It's causing quite the tension between Coach Randall and Coach Hall."

"How so?"

"Randall is the academy coach and Hall is our high

school coach. Now Randall thinks Hall had something to do with the kidnapping. Randall already had superstar Astrid but he managed to convince several more promising local athletes to quit the high school team and join the academy. Hall swears Randall bribed the girls, so Randall now thinks Hall tried to ruin him by arranging the kidnapping, especially because Astrid wants to go home now."

"Do you think that's a possibility?"

"I don't know what to think anymore. After accepting the position as mayor, I've learned that desperate people do crazy things."

"You have no idea the things I've seen," Gunner said. "I'll look into this and report back as soon as I get word."

* * *

EMMA PULLED into the parking lot of one of Coldwater Cove's parks. Harry's car was there, next to the trail leading into the woods. She watched him gather his camera equipment and walk down the path until she couldn't see him anymore.

Quickly climbing out of her rental car, she headed toward the trail. A few other cars were parked with people hiking, skiing, snowmobiling, and dog sledding now that the storm was over. They had different trails for different activities. Harry chose the walking trail.

Harvey always said natural light was best and pictures came out better when the sun wasn't shining. Today the sky was a little overcast, with the sun peeking through a few spots but not bright and glaring.

It was the perfect day for pictures.

Emma entered the trail and walked for a little bit but didn't see Harry. Snow crunched beneath her feet, the sound echoing loudly. It felt desolate, like she was the only person on the planet. She loved nature, but this trail somehow felt eerie and creeped her out. She didn't want to go too far down the trail for fear that someone wouldn't hear her if something went wrong. She chuckled to herself. What could possibly go wrong?

Harry Smith was *not* a threat physically.

"Why are you following me?" came a male voice from behind her.

She whirled around, startled. "Harry, you scared me." She laid her hand on her chest. "I'm not following you."

"Really," he said dryly, looking way less shy and timid than he did back in high school. "I saw you in my restaurant earlier."

"Look, I needed to clear my head. Stacy asked me to lunch, and I admit, I saw you leave with your camera equipment. That gave me the idea to go for a hike."

He stared at her dress boots suspiciously. "That's not hiking footwear."

"Like I said, I was being spontaneous. I didn't want to return to my hotel room for the proper gear because I only planned on going for a short hike to clear my head before dealing with my parents." She rolled her eyes. "You know how that is."

"No, I can't say that I do." He looked down the trail as if lost in memories for a moment. "My parents died in a car crash right after high school."

"Oh, gosh, I'm so sorry. I didn't know." Emma slapped a hand over her lips. She'd left right after high school, and had only come back once before her college graduation. It had been too painful, so she hadn't been back in the five years since college. She really needed to do her homework before sticking her foot in her mouth.

He shrugged and looked back at her. "They weren't

the nicest people. At least they left me money. I used my inheritance to buy the diner."

"Congrats on that, by the way. The food is really good. Looks like business is booming." She paused a beat before adding, "I hear the kids really like it."

He shifted his stance, and a strand of red hair fell out of his ponytail. She noticed his knuckles turn white as he gripped his equipment. He suddenly didn't look so scrawny anymore. "What are you getting at, Emma?"

She'd struck a nerve.

How interesting. "Nothing." She held up her hands, wondering what had bothered him. "I'm just saying I heard your place is a hangout of theirs. I can see why. You're young and hip. They can probably relate to you. Not to mention it's very generous of you to take pictures of them for free."

"A lot of these kids don't have endorsements yet, so they don't have money for head shots. It's not a bad thing to help people out, Emma." His face hardened. "No one ever helped me out when I was a kid." His eyes met hers and narrowed. "People weren't very nice to me back then."

She'd never been mean to him. She wouldn't do something like that to anyone on purpose, but he also never gave anyone a chance to get to know him. She looked at him with sympathy. "I didn't mean to insinuate it was bad to help these kids out, and I'm sorry no one ever helped you. That had to have been hard on you."

"I don't need your pity." He thrust out his chin. "I'm tougher than I look."

"I'm beginning to see that."

"Well, I gotta go." He adjusted his equipment.

"What are you taking pictures of today?"

"Birds." He looked up into the bare trees.

"In the winter?" She laughed.

"Not all birds migrate."

"Huh. I did not know that. Very cool." She was trying to appeal to his good side before she dropped any bombs.

"In fact, there are quite a few birds that stay in Maine all year long." His genuine enthusiasm was palpable. "Today I'm looking for the American Robin and the Eastern Blue Jay."

"Astrid Westergaard likes birds." Emma gauged his reaction carefully.

"I know." He frowned. "I saw her Blue Jay tattoo once."

"Oh, really? Was that when you photographed her?" She looked at the sky innocently and then at him.

His face hardened. "She wouldn't let me."

"That had to make you mad."

His eyes turned cold, his posture defensive. The years had hardened him. "I don't know what game you're playing, Emma, but I would be careful if I were you. I'm not the weak little boy you once knew."

There was definitely something off about him. "I don't like games, Harry, but you can be sure I'm *always* careful."

A teenage girl she recognized from the academy came walking down the path right up to them. "Hi, Harry. Am I too early? Vanessa had a cancellation, so she finished doing my makeup and hair before I expected. Didn't she do an awesome job? All the girls love her. I hope I get some endorsements after this." The girl smiled bright, full of dreams and aspirations. She couldn't be more than fourteen or fifteen years old.

"I thought you were taking pictures of birds?" Emma raised an eyebrow at him.

"I was, but you used up all my free time. Come on, Shelly, I know a great spot for your headshots." He started walking away.

"Do your parents know you're out here, Shelly?" Emma asked.

Shelly nodded excitedly.

Harry looked over his shoulder back at Emma with narrowed eyes. "I'd say it was a pleasure, but I would be lying. You'd do well to remember what I said earlier." With that, he disappeared down the path, leading Shelly quickly away.

Emma headed back to the parking lot, his words and actions on replay in her mind like a mystery movie. She climbed into her car with one realization that was becoming increasingly clear....

Harry Smith just might be more of a threat than she thought after all.

* * *

GUNNER WAS ABOUT to enter his hotel room when he heard Emma coming down the hall. He paused with his hand on his doorknob and watched her. She looked so good. Her honey blond hair wavy from all the layers and being wind-tossed, and her face sun kissed like she'd been outside for a while. He wondered where she went, but forced himself not to think about that. She wasn't his responsibility anymore.

But that didn't mean he didn't miss her like hell.

They hadn't really spoken since the showdown in the woods. He'd avoided her as much as possible because he didn't trust himself. He'd overreacted. He knew that, but he couldn't help feeling hurt at least a little. He felt too vulnerable around her, but his heart ached without her. He knew if he was near her too long, he would throw caution to the wind and take a chance, risking getting hurt for real.

He remembered the innocent woman and child he hadn't been able to save because of someone he'd trusted with his life who had betrayed him. Emma not telling him about the note was different than what happened before, but she'd still knowingly put them in danger. Unlike the woman and child, Emma wasn't a stranger.

If he lost her, he would never recover.

He'd opened a small space in his heart, and she'd filled it to overflowing. Their physical connection had somehow touched his soul. She made him feel alive and, for the first time, he'd believed he could beat the demons which had haunted him for so long. But she'd broken his trust.

That hurt even worse because he could admit he was in love with her.

"Hi, Emma," he spoke after it was obvious she hadn't seen him yet. He missed talking to her more than he cared to admit.

She jumped, and her face flushed crimson. "Gunner." His name came out on a breathy whisper that affected him in ways he couldn't afford to act on, no matter how much he might want to. "Sorry, hi. I didn't see you there."

He cleared his throat. "I didn't mean to scare you."

"It's okay." Her eyes filled with longing and a little bit of sadness. "How have you been?"

"Okay." He kept his face unreadable. "You?" He couldn't let her see this small talk was killing him after all they had shared. His battered walls couldn't take much more.

"Just trying to get through one day at a time. I won't rest easy until the leader is caught." There was an awkward pause between them, and she began to fidget. "I went for a hike today."

That explained her wind-blown look. "I'm surprised you would want to go back into the woods so soon." He glanced at her dress boots and raised a brow.

She saw him looking at her footwear. "I didn't really, but I saw Harry Smith with his camera, so I followed him."

Gunner's gaze snapped up to hers. "Why?"

"I had a few questions I wanted to ask him about Astrid."

"The sheriff is investigating the case." He left the words *haven't you learned anything* unsaid, but it was clear she'd read his mind.

"I was being careful," she said, her tone defensive. "I stayed close to the parking lot, within earshot of others."

He held up his hands. "Never mind. That's not my business anymore." He had to stop trying to protect her. She'd made it clear she didn't trust him fully, or she would have told him everything up front.

"I want to tell you," Emma said softly, and her words *just like I wanted to tell you before* went left unsaid.

It didn't matter. The damage had already been done.

"I went to high school with Harry but didn't know him that well," Emma continued when Gunner remained silent. Stacy mentioned he takes pictures of the kids and that he was pretty impressed by Astrid, but she didn't give him the time of day. I thought maybe I could get something out of him since we went to school together. That maybe he would slip up and tell me if he kidnapped Astrid to scare her and teach her a lesson."

"Did he tell you anything?"

Emma shook her head. "No, unfortunately, but there's definitely something off about him. A girl from the academy showed up early for some headshots. He gave me a weird warning before I left. What do you think we should do?" She looked at him with hope and something he didn't want to identify shining bright in her beautiful green eyes.

Gunner hesitated a moment but then said, "I think *you* should tell Trent. I'll be leaving soon."

"Oh." Her face fell. "When?"

"In a day or two. I'm finishing up something for the mayor and helping your brother a little more at the pub before I go."

Her eyes widened with curiosity. "What are you doing for the mayor?"

"I can't talk about it."

"I see." She straightened her shoulders. "Thanks again for everything you've done for me and my family. I hope you find whatever it is you're looking for." He could tell by her tone and body language that he'd hurt her.

He relented a little. "That's just it. I don't know what I'm looking for. No place feels like home anymore." He pinched the bridge of his nose and sighed. "What do you want from me, Emma?"

"Nothing you don't want to give. Don't worry about me, Gunner. I'm not your business anymore, remember?" She stepped through the door to her hotel room and closed it behind her with a resounding click, and he feared she just might have closed the door to her heart as well. This was what he wanted, wasn't it?

Then why the hell did it feel like his insides were tearing apart?

18

"WHERE THE HELL IS BART?" Jack asked his father as he came out of the kitchen in The Claw.

He'd called Gunner and asked him if he could try to find the maintenance man before this evening turned into another disaster. The dinner rush would start soon. Even though it was winter and most people hibernated during that cold, dreary time of year, the nor'easter had affected many. They were relying on the local restaurants to provide for them while they recovered from the blizzard and had their homes fixed.

"You have to be patient, son," Bill replied, squeezing his shoulder. "Bart is the only maintenance man Coldwater Cove has. He's working his way through town, I'm sure."

"I get that, Dad, but he's been out of contact a lot lately. Usually, we can still at least reach him and get an idea of when he will be free to stop over. Considering our pub is feeding half the residents dinner, you would think we'd be a priority."

His father rubbed a hand over the top of his bald head and then snapped his fingers. "What about Gary?"

Jack was already shaking his head. "That won't

work. He's a builder. He doesn't fix these high-end appliances."

"Don't stress, Jack. As long as we can serve the folks something cold to drink and your mother's clam chowder, people will be happy."

"I've been making some all day." His mother walked by them carrying a huge crock into the kitchen. Moments later, she joined them. "I have lots more where that came from. Emma and her friends are helping me bring it over."

Right on cue, Emma and JoJo carried in two more crocks and stored them in the kitchen, joining them when they were done.

"I hope it will be enough," Jack said. "What about bread?"

Harvey lumbered in and walked with a cane, limping over to the bar while carrying a huge bag of bread loaves. JoJo came out of the kitchen, planted a kiss on the man's cheek, snatched the bread, and then disappeared once more.

That pretty much answered Jack's question on their relationship status. This day just kept getting better and better. Although, Vanessa kept coming around lately. She'd graduated high school the same year as him. His mother seemed to think she had a thing for him.

She'd always been part of the pageant world. Her mother had been obsessed. Then Vanessa finally hit it big when she won the Miss USA pageant. She'd traveled the world for a year, and he honestly hadn't expected her to return to the Cove ever again. But when her parents retired to Florida, she came home and took over their house, opening a salon in the front.

Growing older tended to do that to a person. Helped them find their roots.

He was four years older than the twins. When he graduated high school, he spent four years in the air force, but after Ellie died the winter of their senior year, when he was home on leave, he decided not to reup. His family needed him, so he'd returned to the Cove when his service was complete and he'd been there ever since.

Maybe Vanessa intended to stay in the Cove for good. Maybe she really did have a thing for him. Maybe it was time he found out. But first, he had to deal with a non-working oven.

"How's the leg?" Jack asked Harvey.

"Better. Thanks for asking and thank you again for helping Jo get me to the hospital." He shook his hand.

"You're very welcome. And very lucky." Jack clapped him on the shoulder. "I've seen a lot, but never anything like that."

"You and me both. I'll gladly stick to storm chasing in the future. I'm walking with a cane now while my leg heals. I should be good to go for next season. I only wish I could pay you back somehow."

"I know how." JoJo appeared from out of nowhere, slipping beneath Harvey's large arm which covered half her torso.

Harvey blinked and then tightened his arm around her midsection as his face transformed into a love-struck sappy smile. The woman was constantly in motion and usually at top speed from what Jack could tell. He couldn't help but grin. Harvey was indeed a lucky man.

"What exactly do you have in mind? Or don't I want to know?" Jack chuckled.

"Let me take a crack at that there fancy contraption in the kitchen for you. It's the least I can do for you helping me save my man."

"That's an oven, not a car," Jack pointed out.

"Look, it's a machine. End of freakin' story." She wiped her hands of the matter as if it were that easy.

"She's right," Harvey said. "My girl can fix anything that runs, basically. She's a phenomenon."

"Aww, Harv, that's about the sweetest thing you've ever said to me. Now let me go, you overgrown sloth. I've got work to do." She slipped out from under his huge arm and buzzed back to the kitchen, disappearing just as quickly.

"Do you really think she can fix the oven?" Jack was skeptical, but at this point he was desperate enough to let her try.

"Trust me, big brother, JoJo is a magician when it comes to any kind of machine." Emma joined them. "Even if she's never seen a particular machine, it doesn't matter. Give her an hour, and she will be able to tell you anything you want to know about it. Where it was made, how to operate it, how to fix it. She's that good."

"If she's able to fix the oven, I'll give her a big 'ole kiss."

Harvey scowled.

"Kidding. I won't, of course." Jack tapped the bar twice.

"Where's Gunner?" Emma looked around. "I thought he'd be helping you. At least that's what he said he was going to do."

"And he is." Jack studied his sister. Something had been bothering her since their ordeal in the woods. "Bart is MIA, so I asked Gunner to see if he could track him down."

"Ah. I see," was all she said, but her tense body language spoke volumes.

A little while later, she was still too quiet for his liking.

"Em, are you okay?" Jack asked. "What's going on with you and Gunner?"

"Absolutely nothing." She smiled a little too wide.

Jack gentled his tone. "Are you good with that?"

"Apparently I have to be." Her eyes were a little too shiny as if she were holding back tears.

"Em, if you want me to—"

"Tada!" JoJo waltzed out of the kitchen, wearing oven mitts that swallowed her arms. "That bitch is fixed."

The pub erupted into cheers.

"That's my cue," Emma said and started walking away.

"Not so fast. You're not off the hook yet," Jack hollered after her.

"Yo, Top Gun, get on over here and feed the filthy animal," JoJo hollered. "She's roaring like a lion and ready to eat. You can talk your sister's ear off anytime. You've got hungry patrons, including Moi."

"You're saved by the crazy lady, Emma." Jack pointed at JoJo and headed for the kitchen.

The pub door swung open and Gunner walked in, dragging a red-faced Bart with him. The whole place grew silent and everyone stared.

"Found Bart," Gunner said to Jack.

Bart didn't say a word, just stared at the floor.

"I see that," Jack replied. "Where was he?"

"In bed with Clark Ford's wife, Betty."

* * *

THE NEXT DAY Emma and Gunner both got called to the sheriff's office. They each sat in a chair across from Trent's desk. They faced front not looking at each other. Trent and Stacy had their heads bent together, going over their notes. They finally sat up and looked at each of them for a full minute.

Trent started. He stared directly into Emma's eyes, reading her every twitch, making her squirm. "Ms.

Ross, why did you follow Harry Smith into the woods yesterday after you had lunch with my wife?"

"Because I felt like stretching my legs."

Gunner coughed.

Emma looked up at the ceiling and counted to ten.

"I see. It had nothing to do with the fact that my wife shared details with you that she probably shouldn't have?"

Stacy shrugged and mouthed *sorry* to Emma.

"We were just having a discussion about how good Harry's restaurant was and that the kids liked hanging out there."

The sheriff motioned for her to keep going.

Emma sighed. "And that Astrid shunned him when he offered to take her photo. It's probably not a big deal. Teenagers are hormonal creatures. That's not really surprising."

"Ah, but you thought it was a big deal to someone like Harry, didn't you?"

"Maybe."

He met her gaze, his unwavering. "Do you trust me?"

"Sure, I guess."

"Then why won't you let me do my job?" He scrubbed his hands through his hair.

"I was only trying to help."

"Well don't." He shook his head.

"I understand how you feel," Stacy said. "I didn't trust the police before I meant Trent, and I got myself into a bit of trouble as well, but he really is different. He will do everything in his power to get to the bottom of this. I can promise you that."

"I tried to tell her." Gunner held up his hands. "She doesn't listen. Or have common sense."

"Neither do you, apparently," the sheriff said, clearly frustrated.

Gunner didn't move an inch, but his eyes narrowed slightly.

Emma snorted, then pressed her lips together. She couldn't help it. Mr. High and Mighty was in trouble for once, and she was enjoying herself immensely.

"What sense did it make for you to drag Bart into the pub and announce to half the town that he was having an affair with Betty Ford?" Trent grunted.

"I was helping a friend out." Gunner's tone was flat and matter-of-fact, as if he were recalling his training on how to answer questions when being interrogated by the enemy.

"I repeat. Don't." Trent took a deep breath, blew it out slowly, and then looked Gunner in the eye. "Your time would be better spent focusing on the matter Mayor Flemming spoke with you about."

Emma's gaze shot between the two of them as a look of understanding passed between them. What the heck was going on?

"Done." Gunner stood. "Is there anything else you need from me, Sheriff?"

"No, and Gunner," Trent paused until Gunner looked at him, "thank you. Your help means more than you know."

Gunner nodded once, and then he was gone.

Emma stood and stretched. "Well, I'll be going now, too."

"Not so fast," the sheriff said, his eyes almost as intense as Gunner's.

Emma sat back down slowly, looking at his wife for help. "Stacy?"

Stacy gave her husband an *At ease, soldier!* look. "It's okay, Emma. I just have a few questions for you. After you rescued Astrid from the woods, did she mention anything at all about Mandy Ford?"

Emma thought about that. She'd had time on the

ride back to town with the rescue teams. Astrid had insisted on riding with Emma because she didn't trust men. Emma couldn't blame her after all she'd been through. The poor girl was so traumatized.

"She did say that her dad thought that Mandy's father had hired thugs to kidnap her to take her out of the competition. She and Mandy have never gotten along. She said she tried to be friends with all of the girls when she first got there. That it was so hard being a foreigner joining a US ski academy because that put a target on her back right from the start. But Mandy out of all of them had been the most jealous. She felt threatened and made Astrid's life miserable from day one. Mandy was the next best skier after Astrid, so they were always neck and neck in the competitions. Astrid wants to go home, so she thinks Mandy and her father's plan worked. They got what they wanted."

"And what do you think?" Stacy asked.

"Honestly, I have no idea what to think anymore." Emma looked at Stacy. "Am I free to go now? I'm getting a headache."

"I can relate." She reached out and squeezed Emma's hand. "Thank you, Emma. You've been more help than you know."

Emma left Trent's office with more questions than when she had arrived. What exactly was Gunner up to for the sheriff and the mayor? And why all the questions about Mandy and her father?

Instead of going back to her hotel room where she might see Gunner and her friends, or facing Jack at the pub, she decided she needed a slice of home. She headed for her parents' old colonial in downtown Coldwater Cove.

Several minutes later, she arrived at their house. This was the house she'd grown up in. The house her brother had lived in. The house where she'd shared a room with Ellie. She literally hadn't been back since she'd graduated college and had moved to Virginia to start her life over.

She pulled into their drive and cut the engine to her rental car. She had to take several deep breaths before she got the nerve to walk inside. She didn't knock. That felt weird. It didn't matter how long she'd been away; this place was still her home. She turned the knob and smiled. Some things never changed. People never locked their doors in this town. She walked inside and had to catch her breath.

Time stood still.

Everything felt exactly the same. They hadn't changed a single thing in all these years. Her eyes were drawn to the staircase leading up to their bedrooms. She could hear the TV on in the living room. Her parents always watched the evening news. She would let them know she was here in a minute.

This was for her.

Emma held the railing for support and because her sister's hand had once touched the same wood, it was somehow comforting. She walked slowly up the stairs and saw three bedrooms. Her parents' master bedroom was to the right. She peeked inside and was comforted to see it still looked the same.

They were the one steady thing she could always count on to never change.

Her brother's bedroom was in the middle. She looked through the door and was pleased to see they'd at least added a desk. The room would serve as a guest bedroom but also an office. Taking a deep breath, she finally made her way to the end of the hall.

Why was this so hard?

Her sister had been gone for a long time now, but being home made everything feel like yesterday. She took a deep breath and pushed the door open. A smile lit up her face, and tears overflowed. She didn't feel sad. She felt grateful. Her sister's things surrounded her, making her feel her sister's embrace. She walked around touching everything and feeling closer to Ellie than she had in a long time.

Except when she'd needed saving.

Emma had felt her sister's presence strongly during those times. It was comforting, knowing Ellie would be with her always. Emma picked up a bracelet that Ellie had always worn. It was her favorite. She slipped it on her wrist and felt comforted immediately.

"What? No! This isn't good," Emma's mother said from downstairs.

"What in the hell is happening to our poor town?" her father added.

Emma went running downstairs, and both her parents screamed.

"Ellie?" her mom croaked.

"Jesus, Mary, and Joseph." Her father made the sign of the cross.

"No, no, no!" Emma held her hands in front of her. "I'm so sorry. It's just me. Emma." She smiled on a cringe.

"Well, I can see that now, but young lady, you scared me half to death for a moment there." Her mother fanned her face.

"You know I'm always glad to see my Bean, but honey, you swore you would never step foot in this house again without your sister," her father added, looking shellshocked. "You do know you were identical twins, right? I know it's been a long time, but you just took a good ten years off my life."

"What can I say? The spirit moved me." Emma sat on the couch by her mother. "What I want to know is what is no good for our town? What the heck happened?"

Her father looked her square in the eye. "Stacy Buchannan-West just announced that Mandy Ford has been kicked out of the academy and off their ski team."

"What on earth for?" Emma asked.

"Using steroids," her father answered.

"And that's not all," her mother added.

"Do I even want to know?"

"Clark Ford has just been arrested for buying the steroids two town's over. Guess we know why he was out of town after the storm cleared."

"To get more drugs for his daughter." Her father frowned.

"No wonder Betty had an affair." Emma shook her head, having no idea how to process everything she'd just heard.

19

"ARE you sure you guys have to leave?" Emma asked Harvey and JoJo the next day out in front of the community center as she helped them pack up The Beast.

"No offense, Em, but your town is crazier than I am." JoJo lifted the hood and checked the engine over one last time.

"Coldwater Cove didn't used to be this way. I have to admit a lot has changed since I've been gone, but the sheriff says things are slowly getting better."

"What's gonna happen to that poor girl, Mandy?" JoJo asked. "We all know her crazy father was the one pushing the drugs on her. I'm glad he was arrested."

"Stacy said her mother is going to homeschool her. She's filing for divorce and ended things with Bart. I think she and her daughter are going to focus on healing. I just hope Mandy gets to ski again. Stacy said, even without the drugs, she was a brilliant skier."

"What about Astrid?" Harvey asked as he scraped the ice off the windows of The Beast. "That poor kid has been through so much."

"She sure has," Emma agreed. "Her father is taking her home to Sweden. She's taking a break from skiing as well. I heard he's planning an intervention and making his wife go to a fancy rehab place there."

"From what I've seen, the man cares more about his reputation than his family." Harvey scoffed.

"Either way, it's good she'll get the help she needs." Emma closed the hatch to The Beast. "There, that's everything. I'm going to miss you two."

"Us too, but the storm is over and you're safe," Harvey said, wrapping her in his big strong arms and giving her a hug. "Plus, I wouldn't mind spending a few days alone with my girl before you get back," he added for her ears only.

She whispered back, "You got it. Take good care of her."

"You know it," he said as he pulled back.

"I sure do, and don't you forget it." JoJo slapped him on the fanny and let out a laugh over his eye roll.

"Are we ready, woman?"

"Let's roll, Romeo. See you later, Em." JoJo gave Emma a hug, whispering for her ears only, "Take your time."

"Will do," Emma replied, then stepped back. "Drive safe."

JoJo saluted and then she and Harvey disappeared in The Beast and drove off, way too fast, of course.

Emma wondered if maybe it was time to get her own place. Clearly her teammates were in love. She couldn't help feeling envious. She would give anything to drive off with Gunner, but that wasn't likely to happen. He didn't trust her and didn't want a relationship with her.

She wasn't his business anymore.

That hurt like hell. In the short span of time since she'd met him, he'd become her world. Her protector, her lover, her confidant. She knew the moment he'd confided in her about his past, that her secret would hurt him. But she hadn't expected him to overreact the way that he did. She didn't have a choice.

She would never have risked Astrid's life.

Deep down Emma had thought for sure he would understand. She'd expected his anger and had been ready to explain. What she didn't anticipate was the level of pain she'd seen in his eyes he'd been unable to hide, nor the shutdown that followed. She wanted to break down his walls because she knew for certain she'd fallen in love with him. It didn't matter now because she couldn't tell him. She didn't want anything from him that he wasn't freely willing to give to her.

And she certainly didn't want less than one hundred percent of his heart.

Emma rubbed the ache in her chest and walked back into the community center, where groups had congregated to work through this latest hit to the town's reputation. The mayor and the sheriff were setting up at the podium for an announcement.

"What do you think is going on?" Emma asked Jack and her parents.

Jack shrugged. "I have no clue. Maybe it's about Clark Ford getting arrested and the whole steroid fiasco involving his daughter."

"I doubt it," their mother said. "That's old news in a town this small. We certainly don't need a formal announcement. Everyone has heard about that by now."

"Maybe they're going to announce that he hired a couple of thugs to take Astrid out of the competition ring." Her father held up his hands. "Who knows? All I know for certain is that Coldwater Cove can't take any more scandals. No one's going to want to move here or visit after all this, and we depend on the tourist season every summer."

"I hear you, Pop, but you'll all have to excuse me." Jack stared at the door. "I have to see a lady about a haircut."

Their mother looked at the door, smiled and waved at Vanessa, and then winked at Jack as he took off in that direction.

Their father chuckled. "Go get her, son."

Looked like everyone was getting exactly what they wanted except for her, Emma thought. Just then, the object of her desire walked through the front door. Her heart skipped a beat and for a moment, she thought he had come to see her.

Gunner's gaze briefly settled on her, then he nodded at her parents and kept walking until he reached Sheriff West and Mayor Flemming. The three of them stood talking for what felt like forever but was probably only around ten minutes.

Emma frowned.

Her gut told her their conversation had to do with the mysterious announcement, but why was Gunner involved? It didn't make any sense. What did he know that he wasn't telling her? Her stomach churned with nerves and the ache in her chest returned. He had no reason to tell her anything now.

Laura finally stepped up to the podium and tested the microphone. It squealed, and everyone winced. Bart made a quick adjustment, and then she smiled at the crowd with the sheriff on one side and Gunner on the other, shoulders squared and back straight, standing at attention.

"Thank you all for coming here today. I know everyone is busy, so I won't keep you long, but we felt this was important enough it warranted a warning."

Warning? What on earth for? Emma glanced at the crowd who seemed equally as confused as her.

"Our investigation into the kidnappers has turned up new information. These men are not related to Clark Ford and the competitive ski ring as some of you suspected, nor are they related to Haanes Westergaard's questionable business dealings." Laura looked around the crowd.

Mumbles reverberated throughout the room.

She held up her hand for silence. "I understand we're all nervous, knowing the person behind the kidnappings is still at large, and it turns out we have every right to be. I'll turn the microphone over to Sheriff West to explain the rest in better detail." She stepped down and took Trent's spot.

Trent cleared his throat. "Good afternoon, everyone. I'm not here to beat around the bush. I'm here to give you the facts before any stories get twisted around. I don't want you all to panic, but it has come to our attention that the kidnappers, Boris and Nikolai, were in fact linked to a human sex trafficking ring."

Gasps rang out throughout the room and voices raised.

Trent held up his hands. "Please, everyone, quiet down and hear me out."

The room settled.

"Reliable sources pinpointed this isn't just an interstate trafficking ring. These men were part of a nationwide organized crime network where they traffic young girls between the ages of twelve and seventeen internationally to areas like Asia, the Middle East and Western Europe. The people who buy these girls have money and extremely high tastes. They prefer fresh faced quality girls like Astrid. Her platinum blond hair and sky-blue eyes would have fetched a high price." His gaze locked onto Emma's, and he tipped his hat to her. "If Ms. Ross and Mr. Nash hadn't caught up to Astrid when they did, we never would have seen her again."

Emma nodded back, more relieved than ever that they'd reached Astrid in time.

"These groups are violent, highly organized, and move swiftly," the sheriff continued. "Educate your children to be alert, travel together in groups, don't go anywhere with a stranger, and don't believe everything people tell you. We've stepped up our search for the organizer of this trafficking ring." He let his gaze travel over all the faces staring back at him.

People started eyeing each other uneasily.

Then he ended in a tone that was both serious and confident, "Rest assured, if you're still in town, we *will* find you."

* * *

A CHILL SLITHERED through me over the sheriff's words. How did they discover the link to the human sex trafficking ring? It had taken me a long time to work my way up into this established ring. Years of my life wasted.

I was *not* going down without a fight.

I started feeling short of breath. I had to pull my shit together. People were looking at me funny, including that bitch, Emma Ross. I forced myself to calm down. Be rational. People were looking at everyone funny after the sheriff dropped his little bomb and made everyone suspicious of each other.

I was a pro. I'd done a good job of covering my tracks. They would never find out who I was. I deserved what was coming to me after all I had been through. Now that Astrid had gotten away, I would have to come up with a new girl who would meet the high standards of my clientele. A girl who wouldn't draw so much attention next time. It wouldn't be hard to lure another one into my trap. I was good at that.

Everyone liked me.

The sheriff didn't scare me. This was my town before his. I just needed to bide my time and let things blow over. Outsiders needed to leave, and locals who no longer belonged here needed to go away again. Then I would start over. I was patient. I'd always had to wait for things I deserved.

If it wasn't for Emma Ross, no one would have gone after the girl until the storm was over. And then it would have been too late. Then she had to go and get that giant Navy Seal involved. He'd talked to the mayor and the sheriff and he was on the stage with them. He had to have something to do with how they found out about the trafficking ring. The meddling bitch deserved something just like I did, all right.

She deserved to pay.

* * *

EMMA COULDN'T STOP LOOKING over her shoulder. Now more than ever she felt herself being watched. Maybe she was just being paranoid after learning there was a human sex trafficking ring going on, and its ringleader was still loose.

She wasn't worried about getting taken herself. She was too old for those perverts' tastes. But she had a feeling the ringleader wouldn't be too happy with her and might even try to get payback by killing her.

Emma arrived at The Lost Horizon right on time for dinner. She hadn't wanted to face Gunner at her family's pub or at the hotel, but she didn't really want to be alone, either. Harvey and JoJo were gone, so Emma had asked Stacy to meet her this time.

The place was crowded with everyone talking about the news they'd heard. The only table left was one near the kitchen, bathroom, and office.

"Thank you for joining me," Emma said to Stacy.

"Well, thanks for asking me." Stacy smiled. "It's nice to have another friend in town. Laura is so busy with her duties. We don't get as much time as I would like together."

"Speaking of Laura, is there any more information you know that I don't?" Emma looked her menu over, then glanced up when Stacy paused.

"I like you a lot, Emma, but I learned my lesson. Trent would be very disappointed if I revealed any more pillow talk."

"Understood." Emma smiled.

Their waitress arrived and took their orders of fish and chips and beer.

"For the record, I like you, too," Emma said, sipping her beer that had blessedly come right away. "Now that JoJo and Harvey are gone, I don't have anyone except my family to talk to. My mother worries and only wants me to be happy, so I don't want to burden her by telling her I'm not."

"I heard." Stacy took a sip of her own beer. "Trent said Gunner is leaving town tomorrow."

Emma closed her eyes for a moment to keep the tears at bay and subconsciously rubbed the ache in her heart, which had become almost constant lately. Why did love have to hurt so much? This was his last night in town, and he hadn't said a word. That spoke volumes. "You know more than I do," she said after a moment of composure. "He didn't tell me what day he was leaving. I wonder if he even planned to say goodbye."

"I'm sure he wouldn't leave without seeing you. You guys have been through so much together. When do you plan to leave?"

Emma shrugged. "I'm not sure. I haven't been home in so long, I figured I would spend a little more time with my family. Plus, Harvey and JoJo won't complain if I give them a few more days alone."

"Those two are so cute together." Stacy sighed dreamily.

Emma laughed. The waitress set their food before them, and they both took a moment to eat. The restaurant didn't disappoint. Her fish was cooked to perfection, golden on the outside, light and flaky throughout. The season salt on the fries was as good as she'd ever had.

Emma finally replied, "I know, they really are adorable. They finally figured it out. Everyone who knew them suspected there was something between them for years, but I never thought they would act on it. I think near death experiences make people find the courage to go after what they want."

"Maybe you should do the same."

Emma shook her head. "It's too late for us. Gunner has too many demons he hasn't made peace with. I feel like I finally made peace with mine."

"I'm glad something positive came out of all this craziness."

"Me, too." Emma stood. "If you'll excuse me, I need to use the restroom."

Stacy waved her off, and Emma headed toward the restroom. She heard voices and stopped to see Bart talking to Harry in his office. Bart was fixing Harry's computer and looked up to catch her staring at them. She turned away and used the restroom, trying not to think about the look on his face.

He'd glared at her with hatred.

What on earth was he so furious with her for. She finally emerged from the restroom only to find him waiting for her. She sucked in a breath and took a step back in the narrow hallway. "Can I help you?"

"Don't you think you've done enough with all of

your *helping?*" he sneered. "I deserved to be happy just like everyone else."

"I never said you didn't."

"I had a good thing going, but you took that away."

"Look, I'm sorry things didn't work the way you wanted, but I didn't have anything to do with that. I'm not judging you, but Betty is a married woman. What did you think would come of that?"

"Their marriage was on the rocks before I came into the picture. You had to go and get that Navy Seal involved. Your meddling made my romance go away. Maybe someone should take away what makes you happy, then you would know how it feels?"

"No worries there, it's already gone."

"Just stay the hell away from me from now on, or you'll be sorry."

"Is that a threat?"

"That's a promise."

Suddenly the lights went out and the restaurant plunged into darkness.

Bart cursed.

Emma tried to find her way back to her table, but she got disoriented in the dark. She ended up in a room when the lights suddenly came back on. She blinked to clear her vision then gasped at the sight before her.

"Harry, is that what I think it is?" Emma stared at his computer screen.

His face paled, and he slammed his laptop closed. "What are you doing in here?"

"I got lost in the dark." She started to back away towards the door, but Harry was too fast for her.

He closed the door and locked it. "You couldn't leave well enough alone, could you, Emma?"

"I won't tell anyone what I saw if you let me go."

"I don't believe you. You blow into town like the prodigal daughter playing hero storm chaser. *I'm* the hero. I spent years building my reputation and making my business a success, and now you want to ruin me."

"If I scream, everyone will hear me."

"No, they won't," he pulled out a gun, "because you're finally going to get exactly what you deserve."

2 0

Gunner had never moved so fast in his life. Stacy had called the pub right after she'd called her husband. She said after the power went out in the restaurant, Emma never returned to her table. Bart got the power back on and said he last saw her by the bathroom. When Stacy searched the restaurant, Harry's office door was locked. What she'd heard through the door scared her into action.

He was holding Emma hostage, threatening to kill her and himself.

Gunner had planned on telling Emma he was leaving for California tomorrow, right after Vanessa cut his hair back to regulation length. But Emma hadn't shown up to The Claw for dinner. He wouldn't leave without saying goodbye to her.

Now he was afraid he would never get to say anything to her ever again.

He barged through The Lost Horizon doors and joined Trent and Stacy outside Harry's office door. Trent had evacuated the restaurant to decrease the chance of casualties during negotiations. Jack stayed back to man the pub while his parents followed Gunner, but they agreed to wait outside after he insisted.

"What's happening?" Gunner asked Stacy in a hushed voice.

"Trent's trying to reason with Harry, but the man is delusional," she whispered.

"Where's Emma?"

"She hasn't said a word."

Gunner's eyes met Stacy's. "What does that mean?"

"I'm not sure, but I'm trying not to fear the worst." She kept twisting her hands together as she looked back at her husband.

"That she's already dead," Gunner said to himself, praying it wasn't true.

What more could his precious Emma go through? What more could *he* go through? If she made it out of this situation alive, he would come clean and tell her exactly how he felt. She hadn't lied to him to deceive him for her own selfish gain. She kept the truth from him because she was told to by this sick bastard in order to save a young girl's life. Gunner had been too caught up in his own demons to admit the truth. A truth that could set him free forever if she felt the same.

For the first time, he felt confident enough to take the chance.

"I can help you, Harry," Trent said in a calm voice, "but you have to put down your gun and open the door."

"I don't believe you. It's a trap. It's not my fault. She wasn't supposed to see. I was so careful. I always cover my tracks. I can't get caught. I won't survive in jail."

"Let Emma go. Cooperate, and your sentence will go much better."

"It's all her fault. This wasn't supposed to happen this way. I didn't do anything wrong. I just look. Girls my own age don't like me. Girls like Emma. They never liked me even back in high school. It's not fair. She's had everything. She should have to pay."

"Emma, can you hear me?" Gunner asked.

The sheriff motioned for him to be quiet, but he couldn't help himself. He had to know.

"Who's that?" Harry yelled.

"Why isn't she talking, Harry?" Trent asked.

"That's for me to know and you to find out," Harry spat.

"If I find out she's dead, I'm coming for you," Gunner growled.

"She's not dead, she's just knocked out," Harry quickly said. "If you come through this door, I will kill her for sure, and you."

"You can try," Gunner said in a deep deadly voice, "but I can promise you, you won't win."

"Easy now, Harry," Trent said, frowning at Gunner.

"I'm done talking," Harry said.

Gunner didn't think for once. He took a page out of Emma's book and simply acted. Throwing himself against the door so hard it splintered off its hinges, he barreled into the room with his weapon draw and pointed right between a startled Harry's eyes.

"I've always felt actions speak louder than words." Gunner cocked his weapon.

Harry dropped his.

The next hour went by with a flurry of movement.

Harry was arrested, Emma was taken to the hospital, Harry's computer was confiscated, and the FBI was called in. It turned out Harry was a pedophile. He had child pornography all over his computer. The ringleader of the human sex trafficking had finally been caught and was going to prison for a very long time.

Gunner felt good about stopping this scumbag from hurting anyone else. He could finally rest easy knowing the streets of Coldwater Cove were safe again. It had been a long time since he'd taken a deep breath. He could see his future clearly now. As soon as Emma woke up, he knew what he had to do…

Put his plan into motion.

***

THE NEXT MORNING Gunner went to Vanessa Taylor's house to get his hair cut as planned. But he didn't plan on leaving town without doing one thing.

Telling Emma he loved her.

Gunner had stayed at the hospital the night before until she regained consciousness, but that hadn't been the time or place to tell her how he felt. Her family was by her side, fussing over her, as well as Stacy and Laura. They'd kept her overnight for observation. As long as nothing took a turn for the worse, they planned to release her today.

And Gunner planned to be ready.

He'd packed his bag because he still had to return to California, but he had a plan to put in motion. And it started with a haircut. Jack had pulled some strings and got Vanessa to squeeze him in.

"Thank you for doing this," Gunner said to Vanessa as she used the clippers expertly around the edge of his hair.

"Thank Jack. I had to reschedule his mother so you could take her spot. Lucky for you, she was more than happy to oblige, all in the name of love." Vanessa winked.

"Yeah, well, we'll see how much love Emma has for me after everything I put her through."

"Have you looked in the mirror?" She looked at his reflection in the mirror before them as she stood behind him working on his hair. "I'm pretty sure you could talk any woman into just about anything from the sound of that baritone voice of yours alone."

Vanessa was a beautiful woman. "I bet you're pretty persuasive yourself. I know you have Jack eating out of your hand."

"I'll admit I usually get what I want." She grabbed a brush and dusted off the back of his neck, then unwrapped the cape from around him.

"It looks great. Thanks again." He reached into the back of his pocket and opened his wallet, then looked down at the bills.

"The pleasure is all mine," she said with an odd tone.

He looked up a little too late as the butt of a gun smashed down onto his head, knocking his lights out.

* * *

EMMA'S PARENTS dropped her off at her hotel room, begging her to pack and go stay with them. She agreed to go later, but first she needed to see Gunner before he left. Stacy told her everything that had happened. He'd risked his life for her, and then he'd stayed at the hospital until she woke up.

Why had he left?

It didn't make sense. Maybe he'd only protected her out of a sense of duty but still didn't trust her. It didn't matter to her anymore. She was through with worrying her love wouldn't be reciprocated and she might get her heart broken.

Her heart was breaking anyway.

She finished packing and then knocked on Gunner's door. No one answered. She knocked again, but still no answer. Glancing at her watch, she realized it was almost checkout time. Her heart sped up. Maybe he'd already checked out and left town. Hurrying, she headed down to the front desk.

"Do you know if Gunner Nash checked out already?" she asked the front desk attendant.

"Yes," the woman answered immediately without having to look. "I would never forget a man like that." She sighed. "I'm sad to see him go."

"Me too," Emma said softly. "You don't happen to know where he went, do you?"

She shook her head no. "Sorry."

Emma walked away from the desk and called her mom from the lobby, but she didn't answer. Her dad never used his cell phone, so she didn't bother with him. So, she dialed her brother. He answered on the first ring.

"What's wrong?"

"Nothing." She couldn't blame her family for being jumpy. She didn't visit for years and then all hell broke loose when she did. "I need a ride, and Mom's not answering."

"I'll be right there."

Within minutes, Jack pulled up to the curb in front of the hotel, and Emma got in.

"How come you're leaving so soon?" he asked as he pulled away from the curb.

"I'm not. It's checkout time and Mom talked me into staying with her and Dad."

"Nice." Jack smiled. "I'm glad you're home, sis."

She smiled back. "Me, too."

His smiled faded. "And I'm so glad that pervert is off the streets."

"Definitely. Me too."

He pulled into the drive of his parents' house. "I gotta get back to the pub. The lunch rush is about to start. Tell Gunner I'll save a bowl of Mom's clam chowder for him."

Emma paused. "I'm not going to be able to do that."

"Why not?"

"Because he left town."

Jack's brows shot up. "I take it your talk didn't go well?"

"What talk?"

"Emma, I don't have time to talk in circles. Gunner went to Vanessa's to get his hair cut, and then he had plans for some grand gesture to tell you how he feels and hope it wasn't too late. So, is it?"

"I wouldn't know because I didn't talk to him." What the heck was going on? Her heart sped up. "You said he went to Vanessa's?"

"Yes, a couple hours ago. Listen, I've got to go. I hope it goes well when you do talk to him. Love you."

"Love you, too," she hollered after him as he drove away.

What. Just. Happened.

She stood there like a fool for a full minute, and then a seed of hope sprouted in her stomach. Maybe it wasn't too late after all. Rushing inside, she dropped her bag and grabbed her mom's keys since they'd turned in her rental car for her.

"Honey, wait, you're not supposed to drive during the first twenty-four hours after a concussion."

"There's no hard and fast rule about that because concussions are different for everyone. I should know. I've had a couple."

"This had better be for something important."

"My nails are a mess. I'm thinking I need a manicure."

Her mother's eyes widened and a grin spread across her face. "Oh, by all means, you must go then."

"Thanks, I think." Emma narrowed her eyes and drove her mother's car to Vanessa's salon. Did everyone know about Gunner's plan except for her?

Maybe that was a good sign.

The seed of hope died when she pulled into Vanessa's driveway. Gunner's car was gone. It looked like she'd missed him again. Maybe they weren't destined to be together because the universe was surely trying to tell them something. She decided to go inside and check just to be sure. Walking through the front door, she looked around but the salon was empty. That was strange.

Usually, Vanessa was fully booked.

"Oh, hi there," she said, emerging from her basement. "I was just putting some of my supplies away before my next customer gets here. Come in, come in." She motioned her further inside. "What can I help you with?"

"I was looking for Gunner, but I don't see his car."

Vanessa walked up front and peeked out, then closed the blinds. "That afternoon sun is so bright, it heats this salon up something fierce." She looked up as if trying to remember. "Let's see, he came in this morning for a haircut, and then he left. Your brother asked me for a favor so sweetly, I couldn't resist accommodating him. I had to cancel your poor mother's appointment to squeeze Gunner in."

So that's how her mother knew.

Emma's heart sank. "Well, I guess he must have changed his mind and left town after all." She started to walk toward the door.

"Awww, you poor thing. Men are useless if you ask me."

Emma looked at her in surprise. "Except for my brother, of course."

"Of course." Vanessa walked toward Emma and backed her up until she fell into a chair. "Here, let me give you a trim on the house. You deserve it, and I think all of us should get what we deserve."

An uneasy feeling came over Emma. "What about your other clients."

"I had a cancellation. It's all good."

"I really don't think—"

"No, you really don't think before you act, do you?" Vanessa pulled out a gun.

Emma gasped. "What are you doing?"

"Giving you what you deserve, which is something my men failed to be able to do."

"You're the ringleader?"

"Abso-fucking-lutely," she sneered, her stunning face twisting into one so evil it was ugly. "You messed up my operation quite nicely."

"What about Harry?"

"That little pervert doesn't have anything to do with my operation."

"Why? I don't understand how you could be involved in something so horrible."

"I worked my whole life to win Miss USA, and then what? Don't get me wrong. Touring for a year was incredible. They treated me like a movie star. But the minute the next year's contestant won, I had to give it all up. They tossed me to the side like trash, and everyone forgot about me. I went from somebody to nobody, with nothing to show for it."

"But look at you now with your thriving salon. Why trafficking?"

"Why not? How do you think I got the startup money?"

"You used my brother." Emma tried anything to get through to her.

"He'll get over it. Men use women all the time." A slice of vulnerability flashed over her face for a moment when she said, "I was raped and they were going to sell me into sex trafficking, but I made them a deal. They would get better use out of my talents by letting me establish my own little corner of the ring."

"I'm sorry for what happened to you, but those poor

girls don't deserve this. You don't have to do this any-more. You could get help."

Her vulnerability disappeared. "I don't need help. I need money. I can get them high quality girls because the girls trust me and worship me like people used to. I worked hard and saved myself. They can do the same if they're clever enough." She shrugged. "Life's a bitch. It's survival of the fittest out there. If they can't survive, then they deserve everything they get. And I'm going to enjoy giving you exactly what you deserve."

"You won't get away with this." Emma had to stall and think of a plan. "I drove my mother's car here. Jack knows I'm here, too."

"Oh, but I've covered all my bases. Your story is so romantic. Gunner got his haircut, intending to make a grand gesture and tell you that he loved you. But being the impatient woman that you are, you had to follow him to tell him how you felt. It was very moving. You both kissed, then he swept you off your feet and drove off into the sunset with you. I saw it all and told you I would let your mother know you were more than fine and would be in touch once you were settled. When you go missing, they'll just assume you're on a grand adventure."

"What did you do with Gunner?" Emma couldn't stop the tears from rolling down her face as the truth hit home. He'd planned to tell her that he loved her, too.

Why were they always too late?

"Don't you worry about him. He's below us if you know what I mean?"

Emma dropped her head to her lap, hanging over her purse, and cried. "You killed him and buried him?" She reached inside her purse and grasped her father's hunting knife, still wailing loudly. Ever since her con-frontation with Harry, she'd started carrying it. She knew what Vanessa meant, all right, and she also knew it was up to her to save them.

"Stop crying like a baby and face your destiny like the grown ass woman you are. I want to see the look in your eye when I shoot you in the head."

Gunner's words came back to Emma. *Cut your attacker long, deep, and accurately. Cut the lower arm, and your attacker can't grab you. Cut the upper arm, and your attacker can't swing an impact weapon. Cut the thigh just above the knee, and your attacker can't move.*

Emma held the knife behind her purse and stood up.

"What are you doing?" Vanessa thrust the gun out before her.

"Facing my destiny like a grown ass woman, bitch!" Emma dropped her purse and lunged forward, cutting Vanessa long and deep across her forearm and then across her upper arm.

Vanessa's face registered her shock. The gun dropped out of her hand, and she stumbled back a step, her face growing paler by the second.

Suddenly, the door burst open and in rushed Jack, Emma's parents, Stacy, and Trent. "Did we miss the big surprise?" Jack held a bottle of champagne.

"Something like that," Emma said, still holding the bloody knife. "Dad, Gunner's in the basement, hopefully still alive. Sheriff, Harry might be a pervert and deserve to go to jail, but Vanessa is far more evil. She's the ringleader."

Her brother dropped the bottle of champagne, which shattered all over the floor, his eyes full of hurt and then filling with hatred as he turned to the sheriff. "Lock this bitch up," Jack repeated the words he'd spoken not long ago through his clenched teeth, "or so help me God, Coldwater Cove will have another murder on its hands."

Emma's father and Gunner came running up the stairs. He was untying the last of the rope from his wrists and had a bloody spot on his head, but other than that, he looked amazing. Only then did Emma cry, drop the knife, and fly into his open arms.

"Emma, I—"

"Hold that thought," she said against his chest.

"Why? I don't want to wait anymore."

She looked up into his handsome face and touched the cleft in his chin. "Well, I want a proper do-over."

He chuckled and kissed her on the lips. "See, I told you good things come to those who wait."

"I'll have a beer, Charlie," Emma said to the bartender at True North Tavern in Norfolk, Virginia.

It felt so good to be back. She'd promised her parents she would make the time to visit more often. Now that Jack had sworn off women and was running The Claw full time, they had officially retired and said they would come see her when she wasn't chasing a storm.

"What about you, Harvey?" Charlie asked. "Your usual?"

"Red wine sounds great," Harvey said, turning to Emma. "The data on the probes you collected from the nor'easter looks promising."

"I'm glad something good came from that chase," Emma said, relieved.

"Scotch on the rocks for me, Charlie," Jo said, joining them.

Harvey patted the seat beside him.

"How's Gunner?" JoJo asked, hopping on the stool next to him.

"Good, I guess. It's been a whirlwind. He had a concussion like me, and then he had to go back to California, but that was a couple weeks ago. Maybe he changed his mind. I'm not sure what's going on."

"Why don't you ask him?" Harvey said.

"I can't. He's not answering his phone." She checked her phone again.

"So that shouldn't stop you from asking him," JoJo added.

"And how do either of you expect me to do that?"

"Because I'm right behind you," came a deep voice that never failed to bring goosebumps to her flesh.

Emma whirled around, her eyes growing huge and her mouth falling open.

"Remember when I said good things come to those who wait?" he asked softly with the most tender smile on his chiseled face.

She nodded, helpless to do anything else.

"It's time," he said.

"For what?" she asked, not recognizing her own voice.

"Your do-over." He took her hands in his own. "Emma Ross, I did change my mind."

She started to cry.

"I changed my mind about not trusting people because I trust you with my life and, more importantly, my heart. I changed my mind about where I wanted to live, and I got transferred to Naval Station Norfolk just to be near you. I love you so much, and I don't want to spend another day without you in my life. Leave the townhouse to Harvey and JoJo and move in with me. What do you say?"

"I say that was one hell of a do-over," she said between sobs. "I love you so much, Gunner Nash." She threw her arms around his neck and kissed his whole face as she whispered, "Yes," before landing on his lips with a promise of what was to come.

He hugged her tight like he never wanted to let her go.

Resting her forehead against his, she said, "Welcome home, baby."

ABOUT THE AUTHOR

Kari Lee Townsend is a National Bestselling Author of mysteries & a tween superhero series. She also writes romance and women's fiction as Kari Lee Harmon. With a background in English education, she's now a full-time writer, wife to her own superhero, mom of 3 sons, 1 darling diva, 1 daughter-in-law & 2 lovable fur babies. These days you'll find her walking her dogs or hard at work on her next story, living a blessed life.

BOOKS BY KARI LEE TOWNSEND

Two Cents of Doom (Kalli Ballas Mystery #2)
Mind Over Murder (Kalli Ballas Mystery #1)

Harmful Habits (Cece Monroe Mystery #1)

Murder in the Meditation (Sunny Meadows Mystery #8)
Chaos and Cold Feet (Sunny Meadows Mystery short story #7)
Hazard in the Horoscope (Sunny Meadows Mystery #6)
Perish in the Palm (Sunny Meadows Mystery #5)
Shenanigans in the Shadows (Sunny Meadows Mystery short story #4)
Trouble in the Tarot (Sunny Meadows Mystery #3)
Corpse in the Crystal Ball (Sunny Meadows Mystery #2)
Tempest in the Tea Leaves (Sunny Meadows Mystery #1)

Rise of the Phenoteens (Digital Diva #2)
Talk to the Hand (Digital Diva #1)

BOOKS BY KARI LEE HARMON

Dark Seas (Coldwater Cove #1)
Frozen Waters (Coldwater Cove #2)

Valley of Secrets
Until Tomorrow

Jingle all the Way (Merry Scroog-mas novella #3)
Sleigh Bells Ring (Merry Scroog-mas novella #2)
Naughty or Nice (Merry Scroog-mas novella #1)

Brook (Lakehouse Treasures novella #4)
Meghan (Lakehouse Treasure novella #3)
Amber (Lakehouse Treasures novella #2)
James (Lakehouse Treasures novella #1)

Sleeping in the Middle (Comfort Club #1)

Love Lessons
Project Produce

Spurred by Fate (Triple R Ranch short story #2)
Destiny Wears Spurs (Triple R Ranch #1)